CAPSULE

A NOVEL

I0631587

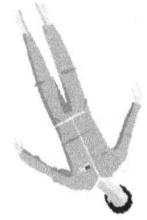

KRISTIN HELLING

CAPSULE
by Kristin Helling

Copyright © 2016 Kristin Helling

Printed in the United States of America
First Printing, 2016
ISBN 978-0-9908743-1-7

Wordwraith Books LLC
705-B SE Melody Lane #149
Lee's Summit, MO 64063

Edited by Ellen Campbell
Cover Design by Corey Helling
Format Design by Kevin G. Summers

e-mail *wordwraiths@gmail.com*
website *www.wordwaiths.com*
Twitter *@Wordwraiths*
Kristin's website *www.kristinhelling.com*

The Library of Congress Cataloging-in-Publication Data is available upon request.

BOOKS BY KRISTIN HELLING

Books available where all books are sold.

THE IDEA MAN TRILOGY

(comedic, suspense thriller)

The Idea Man
The Marked Man
The True Man

THE MASTERMIND MURDERERS SERIES

(psychological, crime thriller)

The Altruism Effect
The Bystander Effect
The Carbon Effect
The Domino Effect

STANDALONE SERIES

(soft sci fi Thriller)
Capsule

Table of Contents

For
Austin,
Rod, Ian, Chris, Caycee, Sarah, and Jeni.
Without you, this book would
not have been possible.

"I said it's a cold universe and I don't mean that meta-phorically. If you go out into space, it's cold. It's really cold and we don't know what's up there. We happen to be in this little pocket where there's a sun. What have we got except love and each other to guard against all that isolation and loneliness?"

David Chase

CHAPTER ONE

Asteroid Mining

Arcturus had done this space walk thousands of times over the years. He had approximately ninety seconds to get his extravehicular mobility unit—his space suit—completely ready for the walk. If he hurried and was ready beforehand, Dex wouldn't have to wait on him. He tightened the straps on his ankles before pulling the boots onto his feet. He'd long known how to put on his suit without assistance, something that had been enforced as part of his training. The torso lay next to him, and as he turned to grab it, he almost leaped out of his skin when a low voice spoke from behind him.

"No. Take it off." Dex stood there in his own EMU, holding the helmet under his arm.

Arcturus whipped around the best he could wearing a puffy suit. The v shaped wrinkle between

Dex's eyes told him that he was serious. This wasn't a joke.

"But Dad, I'm going to have to do all of this on my own someday. Why can't I get the extra practice!? Its not—"

"I said no. I need to do this walk on my own."

A ball of fire began churning in the pit of his stomach. *Not fair! I never have any control!* He thought to himself as he looked away. His anger quickly subsided to disappointment. "I was looking forward to it…" he mumbled.

Dex sighed. "I need you on the inside, yeah? You man the computer."

"The computer is on pilot. It's a routine exterior repair."

Nothing I say will change his mind anyway…

Arcturus already lived almost two and a half decades. This wasn't his first time around the block. And when his dad had his mind made up about something, it was law.

"Just take care of your mother, all right?" Dex asked, his lips thin.

Arcturus avoided his gaze and mumbled under his breath, "Okay. I always do."

Dex nodded, then turned and made his way to

2

the control panel to go through the checklist of things they needed to prep before they could do an exterior repair.

Sulking, Arcturus began the process of taking his extravehicular mobility unit, his EMU back off. Dex finished the checklist faster than he'd finished removing the suit.

Dang, that was fast!

He thought to himself, then brushed it off at the thought that his dad had done this exterior ship repair thousands of times, and he probably knew the checklist like the back of his hand. He turned away as Dex closed the door to the airlock behind him.

It didn't take long for Arcturus to start zoning out as he stared at the numbers on the computer screen. His thoughts were interrupted an hour into the walk, when an alarm rang out from the computer. The shrill sound resonated throughout every muscle of Arcturus' body. This had never happened before.

Something had gone wrong.

From inside the small capsule, he watched the binary numbers on the computer monitor for any reason for the sound that pierced his eardrums. The high-pitched screaming of the system alarm synced with the pulsating beat that erupted in his temples.

"Mom!" he called into his mic.

He'd spent his whole life on the ship *Homeland* in the company of his parents. His mother, Viona, was back on the ship while Arcturus and Dex took a day trip out to go asteroid mining for water to be turned into fuel.

Arcturus' fingers failed him as he tried to hit the button that connected the capsule back to the ship.

"Shit! Mom!" He started to tap away at the computer.

Dex was tucked in a section of the exterior of the ship where none of their cameras could reach. The only information he had regarding the reason for the alarm was the numbers scrolling on the screen in front of him.

The capsule was intact. The alarm had something to do with Dex's EMU. His suit was malfunctioning. Oxygen levels were rapidly declining.

He pressed on the earpiece tucked in his ear. "Dad! Get back to the airlock, now! I repeat. Get back to the capsule."

Nothing.

There was no sound coming in on the receiving end. His communication was shut off.

"Why? No!" His voice was shaky. His body

was shaky. He slid over to another portion of the keyboard.

"Mission Control: come in. Do you hear me?"

"Yes, Arcturus, we hear you."

"I can't get a read on dad. He's still EVA. You have him?" He narrowed his eyes at the screen.

"Arc—it's Zander here. I was just called in. Stand by a moment." Zander was head of their mission at UniX. He was old. And for as long as Arcturus had known him, which was his whole life, he'd looked like an old man.

When Louis Zander was called in, it meant business.

After a moment of silence, Arcturus called back, "Can you tell me what's going on?"

"We're contacting Viona."

"I asked if you had a read on him—"

"Arc! Calm down. Give us a minute!"

He slammed his hands down on the edge of the panel, regretting it immediately after. Sometimes he allowed his emotions to overcome him. His impulsive emotions were mostly a reaction to the very logical and scientific approach his parents always brought to situations. It left him feeling constricted. A feeling he would always rebel against if it were up to him.

He watched as the glowing red digital numbers of the clock counted upward. Fifteen seconds. Thirty seconds. Every blip of the numbers sent a shock through his body. They were taking too long to respond. It felt like an eternity.

And every moment that they took to respond was another moment his father was out there struggling. The UniXplor space station was all the way back on Earth. Viona was back on their ship, *Homeland*. Nobody was here to help Dex.

But I'm here.

He thought as he rose from the seat and headed straight for his EMU. He began to suit up again, even faster and more carelessly than he had before. Just as he locked on his second boot, the computer panel blinked.

His head shot up as the message came in.

"Arcturus. We need you to guide the capsule back to *Homeland*."

His throat constricted at the sound of Zander's raspy voice. He wanted to block out mission control and ignore what they were saying, partly because he didn't want to accept what came next.

"No! You want me to go without him? I'm not leaving!"

Leaving him out here meant leaving him forever. He and his mom and dad were a team. He'd never known anything else. Viona and Dex knew it was a suicide mission, and they'd had this conversation with him before, but it had seemed so far off in his mind.

No. I'm not ready for this. This can't be happening right now!

The frequency erupted and the voice came back through clearly.

"Arcturus. I'm sorry to be the one to have to tell you this, but he's already gone."

Five years later...

Arcturus, knuckles white, tightened his grip on the sides of the gray contoured seat as the capsule juddered. The grapples underneath the belly of the craft buried themselves into the water rich veins inside the body of the asteroid. He sacrificed his hold with his left hand and rested it over his queasy stomach, the muscles in the bicep of his right arm tightening. He forced his chin up and followed the arching surface of the rocky giant. The window of the capsule's flight deck was the only thing that protected him from the vacuum outside.

"Did you track your progress?" Viona's voice crackled in his earpiece.

His stomach lurched up into his throat as his head came in brief contact with the ceiling, which was closer to him than he remembered. He reached up and adjusted the volume on his earpiece before rubbing the crown of his head.

"Yeah Mom, geesh!"

"We can convert the fuel when you're back on the ship. Just collect it for now and get back as soon as possible. Got it?" She spoke quickly, with unsteady inflection in her voice. He sighed, though not loud enough to transmit through to his mother.

"Yup, got it."

"Do I need to remind you that you have an appointment with the therapist when you return?"

"Oh yeah, I forgot about that. I can't make it because I'm busy."

Viona sighed through the transmission. "Busy doing what?"

I knew she wouldn't let me off that easy, he thought to himself as his eyes scanned over the walls of the capsule, trying to think of something he could use as an excuse.

"Mom, I've been talking to a therapist for five

years now. Dad's been gone for five years. Is it really necessary to keep evaluating my mental state? It's like they're *trying* to find something to make up a diagnosis."

In the beginning it was a lot of making sure he didn't feel like it was his fault his father's suit malfunctioned and he lost tether. As time went on, it turned into someone on a computer screen evaluating everything he said and trying to make something of it.

"You will go as long as Dr. Lawlston says you need to." she said.

"Right. I'm gonna get back to work." Before she could speak to him again, Arcturus reached up and removed the earpiece from his ear. He secured the small speaker in a pocket on the side of his thigh.

His hands hovered over the control panel keys, each movement as swift and easy as if he were brushing his teeth. As the capsule continued to mine the asteroid, he looked up at the monitor to see his extraction progress mapped out as a percentage, ignoring the incessant shaking of his chair.

"Thirty-eight percent," he sighed, lacing his fingers together and stretching his arms out in front of him. He yawned as he leaned back. The grumbling of the asteroid drill underneath him in the zero gravity capsule heightened his awareness of the ringing in his ears.

The familiar task reminded him of all the years he spent mining with his father, and he felt intensity in the room that seemed like nothing less than a void. His shoulders tensed as he remembered listening to his father's stories about life on Earth. It had helped pass the time on the boring and tedious, yet necessary, asteroid mining missions.

It wasn't just the thought of being grounded on a planet, it was being able to remain fully exposed to the elements and still be safe. Something he'd only been able to dream about, something he longed for, something he felt robbed of.

He forced a cough as he tried to clear a lump that had suddenly lodged itself in his throat. He turned his head right and left, eyeing the walls of the capsule, only an arm's length away on all sides. And though he'd mined asteroids in this capsule his whole life, he couldn't imagine having to ever be in this craft for more than a day's work at a time.

His breath quickened and he felt a wave of heat creep up his shoulder blades and around his neck. He swiped his hands over his sweat-beaded forehead and weaved his fingers through his curly black hair, frizzing out from the lack of gravity.

"Forty-five percent." His voice trembled this time. Through squinted eyes, the glowing red numbers showing percentage on the monitor had doubled, overlapping each other until he shut his eyelids.

"Mining is never forever. Fifty-five percent more." He exhaled from deep in his chest.

He thought about his mother back on the ship, wondering if she had tried to contact him through the earpiece he'd removed.

I shouldn't have been so disrespectful. He thought. Though just when he was sure she'd been mad at him, she would be pragmatic. Viona never allowed her emotions to show on her sleeve. Whatever frustration she had, she expressed to Arcturus through the amount of chores and tasks she gave him to complete that day. When he got back to *Homeland*, he'd probably have to do more testing and sampling of their stool. It was a shitty job to have. Literally. But he deserved that.

And she'd have to wait, because he had something more important on his mind.

He reached down and slipped his hand inside

the same pocket he'd placed the earpiece, retrieving Viona's contact lens case that lay beside it.

After he unscrewed the circular lids and lowered the case, two clear discs rose in the air. He caught them on his finger and carefully tapped each gel contact over his pupils. It caused an instant dryness, and he squeezed his eyes shut and opened them again, until the contacts rolled naturally with his eye movement.

He looked ahead, his vision now skewed by his mother's saved icons on the desktop of her contacts. His heart pounded in his chest as he searched for her memory data folder, but his curiosity for the truth fueled his actions.

I need to know the reason why I was born to carry out this mission. Why does it have to be me?

If there was anything that surfaced in his being since the death of his father, it was the fact that he was now the man of the ship. It was just his mother and him, and even though she was fully capable of running the entire mission on her own, having done so even when Dex was alive, she wouldn't be around forever either. Most of his training was learning to operate all tasks on the ship. And not because he had a choice.

Because it was a matter of life and death.

His hands trembled at his proximity to a potential answer in Viona's files.

He sifted through a few of her folders, finally giving up and doing a search for memories recorded before or near his date of birth. One file was time stamped just before his parents' launch date. He lifted his hand in the air and tapped the correct icon, then relaxed his muscles and leaned back in his chair.

It took a moment for Arcturus to take in his surroundings. He watched his father Dex pull back a blue velvet curtain and disappear into the flashes of light and media cameras. A UniXplor banner hung on the wall behind a podium on the stage. He spun around as the thick fabric of the curtains whooshed closed behind him. As his field of vision changed, he couldn't control his movements. They were his mother's. All he could do was follow her memory displayed on his retinas.

He tried to shake off the disorientation and followed the visual memory as his mother ran down a long hallway, the click of her flat-bottomed shoes on the tile echoing through the corridor.

She turned; another long hallway of doors lay

ahead. She went to the closest door on the left, waving the palm of her hand over a glowing red circle on the doorframe. The light turned green and the door slid into the wall. It closed swiftly behind her as she walked into the room. As she entered the medical exam room, she walked up to the table that stood in the middle. On the table lay a white robe for her to wear. She surveyed the gadgets scattered throughout the room.

It took a moment for him to comprehend what she was doing, and when he realized she was undressing, he inhaled sharply, closing his eyes to the scene. Since he observed the scene from her eyes, the probability of him actually seeing her undress was low, but he wasn't going to take any chances. The picture went black as he stared into the insides of his eyelids, though he still heard the zipper of his mother's flight suit from the video.

When the video silenced, Arcturus slowly opened his eyes, seeing she had folded her flight suit neatly by the door and was sitting up on the table.

In the quiet room, he heard his mother breathe. In and out. In and out. He tensed up his shoulders. His own mouth felt dry as he listened to her tap her fingernails on the edge of the table. He shifted in his chair as he realized he sat alone here and now, waiting, just as she had all those years ago. He bit his lip as his stomach tightened.

I shouldn't be watching this. If she wanted me to know she would have shown me...

But he continued to watch. He had to know. He had a right to know.

The door slid open.

A straight-spined man wearing a knee length lab coat walked into the room. He had dark hair on his upper lip that wrapped around the chin on his honey colored complexion. He carried himself with grace and ease as the door swooshed closed behind him.

Arcturus recognized Dr. Lawlston immediately, even though he was viewing the man in his youth. He hadn't changed much apart from the fading of his hair and looser features on his face.

Lawlston was wearing a metal contraption on his head, multiple arms extending from the piece. Each metal extension from the headpiece held a medical device: a reflector, a camera, a thermometer, syringes, and any other tools he would need. Behind all the gadgets, he smiled warmly at her.

"Sorry to keep you waiting. I just saw Dex—"

She inhaled. "Did you?" Her voice was higher pitched than usual.

He walked over to the counter and slid open a drawer. He retrieved a few metal tips from the drawer and clanked them down on the counter.

Arcturus could identify one as a light, the others he wasn't sure of. Lawlston reached up and grabbed one of the extenders on his head device and screwed the tip onto it.

"You seem nervous," he said, his back to her. "Have you been keeping to the diet?" he asked, and looked over his shoulder at her.

She nodded her head up and down vigorously. "It's tasteless, though. I don't like that." She spoke in a hushed tone.

He laughed. "Well taste isn't the point. It's just so you get the exact nutrients your body needs to function. When you're up there, you're not going to care about food. Your body will crave what it needs, not what it wants."

"But will my mind?"

He laughed again. "There's the Viona I've been seeing for the past year." Lawlston reached over and grabbed a rolling stool. He sat on it, waved his hand under the bottom to raise it, and pushed himself toward the exam table. "All right, lets get this started. Kind of bittersweet that this will be our last face to face meeting, huh?"

"Yeah, it really is. I'll miss you. I heard the doctors in space aren't as friendly as on Earth." She gave a rueful grin.

Lawlston chuckled as he grabbed a chart from a thin metal tray on a stand, stationed off to the side.

"Go ahead and remove your gown." He adjusted the tray closer to himself.

Viona didn't hesitate at the command, and Arcturus was glad once again that he saw the scene through her eyes, rather than a bird's eye view.

He was fully aware that his parents gave up their right to privacy when they accepted the mission. They could not become astronauts in this day and age without having their entire physical being charted out on scientific grids.

Lawlston reached up and grabbed one of the arms on his headgear, detaching a silver vial connected to a long needle. He used the syringe to draw blood from her forearm, the deep crimson filling up the bottle.

Her health was in the top one hundred percentile. Her weight and muscle mass was exactly to code.

When authorities approved their mission a year ago at the time of her final physical, she had to sign a release form that dedicated her life to it. And if UniXplor was going to spend millions of dollars on an extensive manned mission, they were going to do it right.

Dr. Lawlston was assigned to the mission, chosen for his history and credentials. They placed him in a pool of other doctors, surgeons, and even scientists. He wasn't too excited about creating two super humans, with perfect health and bodies, only to see them die. He'd always contemplated whether or not the cause was important enough. And though he couldn't convince either of his patients otherwise, he supported them because it was his job. If he sent them up in the space capsule and one died of cardiac arrest before the mission was complete, then it would have all been for nothing. He would be disbarred from the medical sector, if not worse. Even though he hadn't wanted to be in the pool to begin with, his name had instantly turned famous.

Next came her vitals. With the devices he had on his head, he checked her pulse, her eyes, and her throat.

"Lay down for me, please." he requested, rolling in his stool to the side of the table.

She let out a long breath, laying back.

After making a few marks on the tablet chart he was holding, he leaned over and set it back on the tray. He placed two metal circles on her abdomen and used his hand to poke and prod her organs, her ribs, and her lungs.

"Take a deep breath," he requested.

She inhaled.

"And out."

Arcturus heard Viona huff into the air as he stared up at the ceiling with her.

"S'cold," she said, referring to the two metal discs on her abdomen, signifying to Arcturus that the temperature must have changed.

Lawlston's headgear began to beep, and he pulled down one of the arms on the device to study the attached screen.

She quickly looked away from his gaze. The sudden movement gave Arcturus a woozy feeling in his stomach.

Lawlston removed the two metal discs from her abdomen and put them off to the side, pushing the screen up to look her in the face.

"Is there something you want to tell me, Viona?" he asked.

She sat up and pulled the robe up over her shoulders, covering her chest and crossing her arms. She shook her head back and forth like a child.

"No... " She spoke just above a whisper.

"I'm detecting levels of chorionic gonadotropin in your system. *High* levels."

She gulped. The science shows everything. And Arcturus had the feeling that she'd known it would.

"Viona, you're pregnant."

A sharp silence thinned the air between them.

"Pregnant!" He stood up and threw his arms in the air.

Arcturus' throat constricted as the doctor voiced the words. He clenched his jaw tightly and balled his hands up into fists, if only to contain his nerves. Though he felt tense as he watched the scene, a sense of relief washed over at the validation that he had found the data recording he was looking for.

"How careful have we been?" Lawlston asked her.

She said nothing at first.

"It's a suicide mission!" He spoke out again,

keeping his eyes fixed on her.

"Sit back down, please?" she asked quietly.

He sat.

"Doctor... I... Dex and I planned this," she said.

He raised an eyebrow, clearly confused.

"C'mon. You know we're going to die up there. We came up with the plan that we would get pregnant, and because we will not be able to bring any information or data home from the mission, we would teach our offspring to do just that. What if the QED fails?"

Offspring. So scientific. So calculated. Arcturus knew that he was a planned pregnancy, his parents had told him that all along. But the way she spoke of him almost as if he was part of an experiment left a metallic taste in his mouth. A sharp pain pierced his inside bottom lip and he realized he had bitten himself; the taste must have been the iron in his blood that gushed in between his closed lips. He swallowed it.

"Have you told UniX?" Lawlston asked quietly.

She shook her head no. "Too much liability. They've put in so much money for this mission."

He stood again. Before he could speak, she cut him off.

"What choice do they have, anyway? They were willing to sign us up and fund us when it was just Dex and I. And everyone knows we don't have the years in us to make a round trip. They were okay with that!"

"I know that you're a practical woman. But you have to think of the morals, Viona. How much would you be depriving this child of? And not giving them a choice? This could go very wrong... " he said.

Well at least somebody thought of me as an actual human life instead of just a way to transfer research. Arcturus listened intently, his legs tingling as if they had fallen asleep from the tension. He began to feel the back of his neck burn, a familiar feeling he got when he was nervous.

"I don't see how raising the baby in *Homeland* could be any different from raising it here on Earth. And there's just a part of me that feels like something is missing. I feel like... I feel as though I will look back on my life and regret all of this if it doesn't amount to something."

Lawlston walked back over and sat on the stool by the exam table. He pinched the bridge of his nose as he closed his eyes. "Bringing a child into this, well galaxy, seems very selfish to me. Parenthood will change you forever. Obviously it's too late to turn back now, but you must realize that your reasons for wanting a child need to be selfless."

"This person sitting in front of you has given up her life for this mission. My intentions are nothing but selfless. This baby will be the most important and cherished being in the entire short span of my life, as well as for the rest of humanity. And I need you of all people on my side, Doctor... because I'm scared, too." Her voice began to crack.

"Who will deliver the baby?" he asked quietly.

"Who do you think?"

"Dex is not trained! If you die, it's on me! We could get in a lot of trouble... and you're not going to be here to suffer the consequences like I am!" Lawlston stood again and began to pace the room. He turned to the counter and removed his head contraption, running a hand through his hair multiple times.

She spoke out, "I've told you so many times. This mission will tell what the future holds for all of mankind. We haven't had the resources to discover it before now. We need you, Dr. Lawlston. Dex has been researching and studying up on how to deliver a child. I trust him. You have to somehow get us the equipment we need onto the ship. And supplies for the life of a third person—food, clothing, medicine. Everything that's on there for us, add more." She waited in silence for him to reply, tension building as the silence created a faint ringing sound in their ears.

"I'm going to go grab ultrasound equipment. I need to make sure that not just you, but that the baby inside you is also healthy. Everything has changed now." He moved over to the computer on the counter and began to type vigorously into it.

"So does that mean you'll help?" she asked.

He stopped typing, his hands hovering over the keyboard a moment. He turned and walked towards the door.

Arcturus already knew the answer.

"I'm going to go notify the officials that the mission will be delayed—"

"No!" she shrieked.

"It *will* be delayed, because you have an abnormal wave pattern in your kidney. Nothing serious, but I need to keep watch on it before I can let you fly," he said slowly, avoiding eye contact.

"I do?" she asked shakily.

"That's what the officials and public will know.

I need more time so I can make sure you and your baby are safe, as well as get that equipment on your ship," he clarified. Before she could speak, he continued, "… that little life inside you, is going to save the future of mankind."

"I sure hope so," she answered.

Arcturus heard her smile through her words.

"Right. I'll be right back." He turned to the door. "And that baby..." He began turning his body slightly from the door, but not looking at her.

"…your baby is going to be the most famous human on Earth."

"Ah!" Arcturus yelled out in the capsule, rubbing at his face as the pain of a sharp object irritated his eye. With the thumb and index finger of his left hand, he reached up and pried open the troubled eye. Holding it wide, he used his other index finger to carefully tap on his pupil, retrieving the clear gel disk that was layered over it. He pulled the contact out and held it up to look at it in the light.

It stuck to his finger, and he squinted his watery eyes as he spotted a small speck of dust on the contact. Balancing the contact, he unbuckled the belt.

He pushed off the chair giving himself the momentum to make it to the wall of the capsule. As he ran his hand along the wall, he gripped the handle of one of the drawers, and reached inside to pull out a bottle of contact solution. Carefully squeezing the bottle in the air over the contact on the pad of his finger, he allowed a droplet to form a bubble at the top of the straw, and then used it to moisten into the contact. He swirled it around.

As the glistening contact clung to his finger, he retrieved the container to secure them back in his pocket.

He maneuvered himself around the chair and grabbed the buckles, then strapped himself in once more and turned his attention to the extraction progress percentage on his monitor. The bar on the screen blinked, and he took the proper measures to retract his equipment.

He let out long sigh, realizing he'd been holding his breath for a moment longer than he meant to. He reached forward to unlatch his helmet from the control panel, pressing it down on his head and feeling inside to enable communication with *Homeland*. As he pressed it to his ear, he heard the white noise of static before his mother's feed came through.

"Where have you been?"

His stomach jolted at her voice and he reached up and grabbed his chest with his hand, not expecting it to be so loud.

"I was uh—I uh—" he began, before she cut him off with a higher screech than normal.

"I've been worried sick! You can't just cut off feed like that."

Okay, maybe she's madder than I thought she'd be.

"Mommm, I've done this a thousand times."

"Don't you shake me off, buddy. Because I brought you into this galaxy and I can take you out!"

He relaxed back in the chair. "Well, that wouldn't be good for anyone." He grinned, and then revved up the capsule's engine, ready to unhitch himself from the beastly rock and head back home to the ship.

CHAPTER TWO

Remembering Dex

The door to the AGC—artificial gravity compressor—slid shut behind him. He reached out and grabbed hold of the wheel on the door, spinning it clockwise until he heard it 'thunk'. As he waited for the hardware to activate, he closed his eyes and brushed his thick hair back with his hands, his finger catching on a tangle. He felt weight beneath his feet, opened his eyes, and spun around as the door opened into his bedroom.

His bedroom was a large octagonal room that appeared very bare. Only a cot-sized bed to the left, a window cut out of the ship on the wall above it. To the right was a wall full of floor to ceiling metal drawers, housing all his things. The ceiling arched into a dome, splashed with the colors of a hand painted mural. Hues of orange and red sprayed from the corner, shooting rays across a marble blue background. Viona told him it was what the sky looked like if you were standing on Earth and looking up as the bright morning sun marked the beginning of a new day. She stressed to him the importance of new beginnings, and that each day he had the ability to make it how he chose.

Two doors stood opposite of the AGC. The first was the toilets, and the second was the door to his parents sleep room. These few rooms before him were the only compartments in *Homeland* that utilized artificial gravity hardware, making it possible to walk in this part of the ship the way you could on Earth.

He left his room and went to his parent's door and slid it open, using the circle sensor on the doorframe. The room before him looked identical to his own, apart from the vaulting ceiling. He headed for the metal drawers inside the wall to his right and knelt down, opening the one closest to the floor.

Just as he reached into his pocket for the contacts, a noise that sounded like the clanking of pipes rang out behind him. He darted a look over his shoulder to the door as the little hairs on the back of his neck pricked up. For a moment he thought he saw a figure standing in the frame, but the vision disappeared almost instantly.

"Man..." he whispered to himself as he dragged the palms of his clammy hands against his pant legs. Kneeling in front of the drawer, he slid it open and dropped Viona's contact lenses into the bottom, right where he found them. He scanned inside the drawer, and right before he was about to close it, a fleck of gold caught his eye.

He reached in and lifted out a white flight suit, a rectangular gold pin fastened to the front. He gathered the fabric in his hands and pulled it to his face, taking a deep whiff of it. He held the suit out in front of him and looked at it. An adult male all white suit, the American flag above the UniXplor flag patches on the arm. He ran his fingers over the patches, following the seam to the front. The pin read *Dex Holst*.

Arcturus scrambled to his feet and quickly unzipped his own suit. He slipped it off his body and kicked his feet out of the legs. He grabbed the white flight suit and pulled it over his legs, clenched his shoulder blades together and bent back to grab the top of the suit. It slipped briskly up over his shoulders and he zipped up the front.

A moment passed while he stood there and felt the energy run through his arms and legs, a heavy weight in the pit of his stomach. The arms and legs fit perfectly, as if it was made for him to begin with.

As he stood in his parents' room trying to remember when his father last wore this exact suit, he heard a throat clear behind him.

He wheeled around, this time seeing his mother unmistakably in the door. She held two silver pouches in her hand and stared at him wide-eyed, stopped dead in her tracks. The hand that held the pouches dangled down to her side, while the other reached up to cover her mouth.

He advanced towards her, reached his hand out, and cautiously grabbed her shoulder.

"Mom... what's wrong?"

"You look... " she began with a catch in her voice.

He looked down at himself. "Oh! I'm sorry... I just thought... since no one is using them anymore that it'd be okay—"

"No—it's okay, Arc," she answered. "It's just, you look so much like your father," she finished.

He let go of her shoulders and backed up. "I didn't mean to upset you." He looked at the floor.

"No, I just miss him. You miss him too?" she

asked through short, choked breaths.

"Yeah, I do."

"Dex wore that suit on our launch day," she told him. His mother rarely, if ever, talked to him about the day they launched from Earth.

His shoulders tensed, and suddenly he felt like an intruder in his father's clothes. He couldn't look up to meet Viona's gaze. When she also refused to make a move, frozen in the doorway, he reached out and guided her over to her bed. She sat down slowly, without his assistance, her breathing ragged.

He watched his mother collect herself as he backed up to the wall and leaned against it for support. He felt conflicted as he looked at her, with the memory he watched just moments before in the capsule still fresh in his mind.

"I remember how happy we were on the day we launched *Homeland*. Dex and I were so young, excited to take on the mission of our lives. Literally." She spoke quietly, her voice just above a whisper, and he watched his Mom stare past him, as if she were speaking more to herself than she was to him.

"Not only was I excited to finally be able to live out the dream I had studied and loved for so long, but we were also going to be having our first child." She stifled a small laugh as she reached up and brushed her hands across her cheekbones.

"There were so many feelings of uncertainty."

He heard himself breathing in the tension of the room. He stole a glance at the drawer he'd dropped her contacts into. He remembered how young she really had been in those memories, and for the first time he noticed the age lines that defined the features of her face. It was as if she took a turn in the direction away from her youth, and he'd never noticed when her age began to have an effect on her.

She stretched her arm out to hand Arcturus the pouches she brought with her.

"Dinner is served," she said, and smiled. She pulled back the lid of the straw on her pouch and sucked out the tasteless, goopy liquid.

He took the meal pouch, and went back to leaning against the wall, holding the silver pouch down by his side. They existed together in silence, the constant low humming of the ship resonating in the background.

"Mom?" he asked, and his voice cracked as he broke the silence.

"Hm?"

His stomach leaped up towards his lungs as for a wild second he wanted to tell her he'd watched her recordings. He chose his words carefully.

"I know that soon you're going to be gone, too... and I'm going to be here alone. You've known this the whole time. And I know that I am going to be the one to transfer the information we collect from outside our galaxy back to Earth... I know all that stuff." He spoke slowly, enunciating every word.

Viona swallowed hard enough for him to hear it.

He continued, "But I just don't really understand what my importance is, other than to do bidding of the people on Earth," he spat out.

She inhaled sharply, "Those people on Earth include you! We are researching for all of mankind. For the future of our race. Searching for G-type stars like Earth's sun that can support M-type planets. We need to find a place for the future, when our solar system is exhausted of all its resources. You know this." She was stern.

She's offended...

He continued, "But haven't you ever thought that the reason we have to search elsewhere for a way to sustain Earth is because those people didn't take care of their own planet?" He continued to poke and prod.

She was quiet a moment. "Sometimes I think about that, too. But it wasn't a specific group of people. It was all of us, everyone," she answered calmly.

"It wasn't me."

"Arcturus Holst!" she scolded.

He ignored her and continued on, "I just think about why, though..." he trailed off.

"Why, what?"

"Well... was I only born to do... this?" He lifted his hands in the air to motion the surroundings of their ship.

"Arc, my child... Most people go through their whole lives lost, searching for meaning and purpose in their existence." She stood up from the bed.

"But you have the most meaningful purpose of all. You have been important to all of mankind, since before you were even born."

He felt her eyes tearing into him.

Why should I have expected any other answer?

His Mom was a practical woman. She looked at everything in scientific terms, requiring reasons for all questions asked. But she was still his Mom. He wondered what the answer to this question would be if he'd asked Zander, head of the mission.

He looked away from her gaze, and walked along the wall, then bent down to grab the suit he left on the ground. He folded it up lopsided and placed it in the open drawer, and then closed it. He chose to leave on his father's flight suit.

"It's almost time for my check-in," he said quietly to Viona, who still stood where he left her. When she didn't say anything, he walked toward the door, and opened it with his palm.

"Eat your dinner," she called to him in a daze.

He looked back at her for just a moment longer and then left, headed for the control room.

Arcturus smoothed out the rest of the meal pouch, pressing the goopy gel between his closed lips. He leaned back in the swivel chair of the control room with his ankles and waist belted in. A simple scan of his hand on the surface in front of him activated the key panel to start up his quantum entanglement device, the QED. The QED acted as the only means of communication back with Earth through real time as *Homeland* moved further and further away.

Light beams shot up to the ceiling as he reached

to the side of the screen and grabbed his headset. The first time he reached for it, he missed, his fingers knocking it further out of his reach. It started to drift, floating up towards the ceiling. With an "Umph!" he snatched it out of the air and pulled it to his head.

"Mission control, this is Arc coming to you from *Homeland.*" He spoke into the cylindrical foam microphone that wrapped down from the headset in front of his lips.

"Pffft. This is 235 to *Homeland,* pfft can you hear me? Pfft."

Static surrounded the words coming through his earpiece. Even the most advanced of technology was still just technology. He adjusted a flat lever on the key panel before trying again.

"Kind... of? This is Arc. Can you hear me?" he replied.

"Oh!... pfft. Yeah, loud and clear! How are you today?" Dr. Lawlston's voice cleared through the static.

"I'm good... though I don't have an image yet—op, there you are. Hey!" He reached up, arm bent at the elbow, and waved in slow motion at the monitor as the image of Lawlston appeared on the screen in front of him.

As Arcturus watched him fidget with several different tablet devices in front of him, he couldn't help but picture the image of Lawlston from his mother's memory. He was older now, his hair as white as the lab coat he wore. He noticed the lines on the sides of Lawlston's mouth, and the apparent bags under his eyes.

"It's great to see you!" Lawlston smiled at him through the screen.

"It's always good to see you guys through this thing... " he replied, pointing over to the QED. "... and even though we're worlds away, you just never know when we're not going to get reception anymore."

"'Ain't that the truth." Lawlston continued the small talk. "Hey, listen. I won't be conducting your check in today. My intern, Diamandis, will be doing it for me. But trust me, you're in good hands." He smiled warmly.

"Sure, okay. I just don't see why I have to do this every single ti—" Arcturus began, when Lawlston cut him off.

"You know this mission is revolutionary for humans and it's necessary we take all the precautions to measure everything that happens to your body while traveling in interstellar space at the speeds you are."

Arcturus watched him explain with tired eyes, a hazy smile on his face.

"Well you asked for an explanation," Lawlston teased, studying his face.

"I pooped twenty-five minutes ago, do you wanna write that on your little chart there?" Arcturus pointed down at the chart Lawlston held in his lap.

Lawlston laughed under his breath and waved somebody off screen over to him. A woman came from the corner, and he followed her body as she walked across the screen to join the doctor.

"Smartass, this is Dia. Dia, smartass."

He felt the back of his neck warm and he tried not to stare as the woman joined Lawlston in the screened image. He observed her long, shiny, wavy blond hair that went past her shoulders and to the center of her back. She was petite, with a doctor's lab coat the same as Lawlston's, and a tablet held up to her chest. She smiled shyly at him through the screen, and the area between his stomach and his chest pounded. He instantly felt the blood rush up to his cheeks.

She leaned over and spoke to Lawlston, saying something he could not hear.

"See you... I'll be back later," Lawlston called out to him.

He felt caught off guard as he refocused his attention. His eyes blurred into a haze before he reached up and waved goodbye to the doctor.

The woman walked up closer to the screen and reached off camera to grab a stool. He observed her grace as she flipped the stool around and situated herself up onto it. Her face was more zoomed in on the screen now, and he noticed that her skin was flawless, with tiny light brown spots that peppered over her nose and cheeks.

"Hello Arcturus." She spoke softly, her voice like a song.

He reached his hand up to his headset and pressed the foam speaker into his ear. He didn't speak at first, but nodded, smiling sheepishly before clearing his throat.

"So. You are uhhh? You're going to uhh..." Suddenly his throat was dry, and he searched around the dashboard for a pouch of water. He felt his underarms rub uncomfortably against the fabric of the white flight suit, and he knew without looking that he was probably sporting some pretty obvious pit stains.

Diamandis wore a small hint of a smile.

"Going to perform your check-in?" she finished for him.

Arcturus nodded, trying to swallow any kind of moisture he could create in his mouth.

"Yes, and we have a lot to go over, so we should get started." She returned back to professionalism, which made him feel more comfortable; he didn't have to worry about being the one to start conversation, which he had never been too good at.

"Can you go ahead and grab the thermometer readers?" she asked, reaching forward and pulling a remote panel close to her chest. She looked up at the screen.

He searched the dashboard with his eyes, and slid the swivel chair fastened down to a track on the floor of the control room. When it locked into place, he unlatched the metal, circular thermometer and pushed the chair back to the center.

"Right. Now please put it in place so I can read your current body temperature."

He did as she asked. He pulled his headset back; still allowing the speakers to stay cushioned on his ears and placed the thermometer on his forehead.

After he turned a switch on the side, the disc suctioned to his skin.

Diamandis looked down at the monitor on her handheld control remote. She bit her lip, watching the machine take his reading.

"Hm... " She continued to look at it. "S'alittle high... " she said under her breath. "Have you been spending a lot of time in the left wing where the paragravity hardware was lagging earlier this month?" she asked.

He shook his head back and forth.

"Hmm... a high temperature could also mean you're nervous... are you nervous?" she speculated, deep in thought as she looked down at her monitor.

"Well, you're really pretty." He heard the words formulate on his lips before he could stop himself. The back of his neck burned again.

She looked up from her tablet at him and laughed under her breath. "Thank you," she breathed, looking back and forth outside the screen. "Why don't we move on to something else and maybe that'll get your numbers back to normal, eh? You can leave the thermometer in place for now though." Her eyes scanned down the chart to the next task.

"We should do a peripheral DEXA to get an accurate reading on your bone density, which is very important."

"Right," he replied, trying to get himself back on track.

"We can perform the scan on your ankle, preferably. Do you have any metal fasteners in that region?" she asked.

"Do I have any metal fasteners on my ankle?" he asked, reiterating the question.

"It'll interfere with the scan." Her mouth was straight.

"Uhh... no... " He reached down and lifted the thin fabric of the white flight suit up to his knee and observed his socks.

"No metal." He confirmed.

"Great." She smiled at him, and continued through the rest of the procedure. As she continued to map out Arcturus's body on her chart, the time with her passed in a blur.

"All right, Arc. I think that's it. Thanks for your cooperation. Any questions for me?" she asked, setting her chart aside and smiling warmly up at him.

He watched the way her eyes creased on the sides when she smiled.

"Yeah, when will I see you again?" he asked

softly, leaning into the camera on the monitor.

What is happening? What are these words coming from my mouth?

He was always the type to sit back and quietly evaluate a situation, apart from those few times that his emotions got the best of him. This time, he was just allowing his words to flow freely from his mouth without a second thought. Sure he'd spoken to people through the QED his entire life, but nobody made him conscious of his words and actions like this woman had.

"Well I'm interning for Lawlston but he's not going to have me on check-in shifts all the time... I can look and see."

I'm just going to go with it. What do I have to lose?

"No." He cut her off.

She looked up into his face through the screen, seemingly taken aback.

He continued, "When can I see you when you're not doing your job?" he asked, clarifying what he'd been thinking since the moment he saw her join Lawlston on his monitor.

"You want to see me again?" she asked, her eyes wide.

"I won't stop thinking about you," he told her.

"Arc... " she breathed.

He watched her closely.

"It's all recorded... " She made excuses, her eyes wandering around the room she was in.

"My whole life is a record, I don't care anymore. For once I just want something real." He held the microphone up to his lips, and caught his muscles shaking, particularly his knees. "But I know I'm probably coming on strong. It's okay if you don't want t... " he began, his voice deepening, when it was her turn to cut him off.

"I want to." She was quick.

"Well then you know where to find me." He looked around the control room.

Go with it. Just go with it.

Something inside him was pushing him to say whatever came to his mind, and the only consolation was Dia's reactions to his attempts.

"Yeah... " she smiled, before she jerked her head to the right, eyeing something off camera. With her mouth slightly open, she relaxed her eyes, and straightened her spine. "Yes... yes wrapping up now," she spoke to them, turning her head back to his camera. "Thank you, Arc. I will be sending your results to the file, and we'll get back with you next time. Mission control signing off." She raised an eyebrow at him.

He stared until the screen went black and she was gone.

He couldn't believe what just happened, though the fact that his heart was pounding in his chest, and that he'd probably need to bring up the levels of hydration in his body from sweating so much, indicated that he may have just experienced one of the best things that'd happened to him, quite possibly ever.

CHAPTER THREE

Brittle Bones

A rcturus hugged his knees to his chest as his head hovered inches above the deck. He stared straight ahead at the upside down control panel. In zero gravity, his body couldn't tell the difference between upside down or right side up, except by the placement of his surroundings.

A lingering high began in his upper chest, the after effects of meeting someone that made the palms of his hands sweaty. Arcturus had spent his entire life in and out of the weightlessness in the ship, but nothing could prepare him for the weightless feeling he experienced after speaking with Diamandis.

He gingerly rotated himself around and stretched his legs out before he looked up towards the red neon light. Near the ceiling of the control room, a rectangular screen lit up several digital numbers counting by the second. It was very easy to lose track of time in his world, where the engine of *Homeland* was continuing to warp space around the ship, allowing them travel at hyper speed, moving light years at a time.

Rather than creating an entirely new way of tracking time and distance, Viona and Dex came to the conclusion that it would be much easier if they followed Earth's time in days and years, all the way down to minutes and seconds. This was also particularly useful for conducting experiments that corresponded with mission control, since the effect of relativity wasn't something they had to be concerned with.

Homeland was set on autopilot, programmed on a particular path, not to be skewed until they reached outside the Milky Way Galaxy. This is where the path would end, though the outskirts of the galaxy were uncharted territory.

And knowing full well that if their calculations about the distance to the edge of the galaxy were correct, Arcturus was soon to celebrate his 30th birthday.

As he looked away from the clock, he saw red dotted apparitions scattering through his vision.

It's been a while since I've heard from Mom...

He rubbed at his eyes and began to make his way towards the door.

Maybe I was a little harsh with the questions earlier. She's giving me space.

"Mom... ?" he called out cautiously. No answer.

"Hmph." He passed through the great room, the door to the asteroid mining capsule, and the long windowed tunnel, cautiously peering in every corner. He began to feel tension building in his stomach, and his gut feeling surfaced.

"Something's wrong." He spoke aloud, his words panic stricken.

He rushed into the AGC and stretched his arms out to press his palms against both sides of the walls. The conversion to gravity couldn't happen quickly enough, and he grabbed at his suit as he felt his heart thump against the inside of his chest cavity.

He was moving so quickly he didn't even feel his feet connect with the floor as the door to his room slid open. Viona was curled up in a ball on the floor with her knees to her head. She whimpered to herself, her body shaking at the curvature of her back in a distinct pattern.

"Mom!" he cried out, rushing to her side and

kneeling down, placing his hand on her shoulder. She inhaled sharply and winced from his touch.

"What happened, Mom, what's wrong?"

"I fell... " she whispered through pained breaths.

"Where do you hurt?" he asked quickly.

"I think... I... it's my shoulder... collarbone maybe?" She sniffled, burying her face in the sleeve of her suit.

"Can you sit up?" he asked, sliding his hand underneath her other arm to help her up.

"Mmyeah... " she breathed, trying to re-situate her body. He was able to get her up to a seated position. She slouched over.

Arcturus' body was very conditioned, and the solid muscles in his biceps tightened as he held up his fragile mother. She had always been a petite woman. Before the mission she was able to build enough muscle mass to qualify her. Though she was nearing her seventies now, and even though aging in space was different from aging on Earth, it was still a cruel reality.

Although technological advances allowed safety measures on ships to include several new ways to reduce exposure to gamma rays and radiation, some of it was still unavoidable, especially considering how long she had been aboard *Homeland*.

They all knew that Viona had been losing bone mass due to the amount of time spent in lack of gravity, and that each and every minute her bones were becoming more brittle, more fragile. Since Arcturus was born in space, his body reacted to the elements of space much differently from his parents, who'd been born and spent most of their life on Earth.

"Oh Mom... " Arcturus breathed, observing her upper back from behind. He could see her shoulder blade poking out abnormally, though it didn't pierce the skin.

"Is it bad?" she asked weakly.

"Yes," he said quietly. His mother was a scientist, and he knew she'd appreciate the truth, if she hadn't known it already.

"I need to reset your shoulder," he told her.

She nodded her head.

He placed one hand on her arm, and the other on her back. He hesitated.

"Do it!" she said through gritted teeth.

"But I don't know how... "

"Now!" she screamed in agony. Without another thought, he pulled back his mother's arm, putting pressure on her back with his other hand. They heard the popping sound of the bone lining back up where it was supposed to be. She turned her face toward him and he saw her eyelids flutter.

"Are you okay? Did I do it right?" he asked frantically. As he let go of her arm from behind, she swayed forward.

"Mom!" He leaped up, moving in front of her to keep her from folding over. Her eyes rolled into the back of her head.

He safely shifted her limp form backwards and placed her head gently on the floor. From this position he scooped up her body and carried her over to his bed by the window.

He balanced himself on the balls of his feet as he crouched down, observing Viona's bandaged shoulder from afar. When he saw her stir, he swiftly went to her side. Her eyelids fluttered open, searching the room rapidly before they fell upon him. He held a small light that fit in the palm of his hand up to her eyes and flickered it back and forth between the two, watching her pupils contract. She scrunched up her nose and turned her head away from the light.

"You want to tell me what's going on?" he asked, dropping the flashlight to his side. Viona sighed deeply and attempted to move her body sideways, moaning from the pain in her shoulder.

"I fell."

"From where, Mom?"

"I was trying to reach the bulb for the ceiling track lights. They're not dimming correctly."

"Nobody breaks their shoulder falling from less than five feet." His mouth was thin, and he kept his composure.

"Nothing is wrong, sweetie." She smiled, her eyelids half open, and she reached up to touch his cheek.

He moved back just enough to be out of her reach.

"Tell me the truth. I'm not a child. And maybe I can help you?" Immediately he regretted his disrespectful response and felt guilt circle inside, settling as a lump in his throat. She stubbornly pursed her lips, shutting her eyes as if it was the only way she could escape his interrogation.

"You can't protect me forever," he said quietly.

She turned her head sharply to look at him. "Yes, I can. And whether you like it or not, you will always be my child. Listen. I'm old. I've studied the side effects of interstellar space on a human body with you remember? And it's against nature for this old body to be away from an atmosphere for so long. I'm losing bone mass by the day. It's obvious. Look at me!" She brushed her hand over her petite body in the bed. It was apparent she was thinning out.

"My bones are brittle," she finished.

He moved himself from the edge of the bed to the floor. He kneeled by her side, observing his bandage-wrapping job on her shoulder again.

"How quickly can your shoulder heal?" he asked quietly, his eyebrows furrowed from concern.

"Guess we'll find out," she answered.

"We need to do a jump." Hoarseness prickled the inside of his throat.

"Absolutely not," Viona responded without a moment of hesitation.

"Doing a distance jump will get us there quicker, and we don't know how much time you will be healthy. We need this—"

"Arcturus. The decision is final. You know it requires too much fuel—fuel that we don't have now that asteroids are scarce as we get further out. We have to reserve what we have!" She was stern with him.

They sat together a moment in silence, listening to the ambient humming of the ship.

"I'm worried about leaving you," she whispered to Arcturus, tears pooling up in her eyes as she lay there, looking out the window above the bed, into the blackness at the passing streams of light.

"Mom... We don't need to talk about it," he breathed. His heart physically felt heavy in his chest.

"You're just like your father. It's okay to be emotional... it's okay to talk about how you feel. Don't bottle everything up."

"I'm happy the way I am. It doesn't bother me to keep things in. And I don't want to talk about losing you. I know it's coming but I don't like to think about it."

He felt her eyes tearing into him, and he fought everything to look back.

"It's perfectly human to die, there's no need to be afraid of it. The thing that concerns me is that even though I knew this would happen when you were born, the fact that we would both be leaving you here alone one day, you're never really prepared for it." She reached up and pressed her index finger into the corner of each eye, sopping up the moisture that threatened to fall.

"Yeah... " He didn't know what to say. He figured it was probably best for him to just keep his mouth shut and let her talk.

"The day you were born, when Dex held you up and I saw you for the first time... It was the happiest day of my life. And I just knew... and your father cradled you in his arms, your little body... and he said, "This tiny human being in my hands... " he said, "You're going to change the world, baby Arc."" She had given up trying to stop her emotions. Lying down, her tears streamed down the side of her temples and onto the bed.

"Mommm... " Arcturus reached up and grabbed her hand, placing his other hand on top of hers. He thought back to his time in the Capsule earlier, how he went behind her back to try and find out her reasons for wanting him. He hadn't realized until now that the feelings he wanted to find can't be recorded on any device.

"You are, Arcturus. And you will change everything for humans on Earth with our discoveries. This mission that has become mine, and has always been your life." She finished to take a breath, sobbing. Her nose leaked onto her upper lip, and she wiped it with the back of the hand that was not holding his.

"I'll try my best... " he whispered, not quite sure what she wanted to hear.

"I have to tell you something." Viona spoke low.

He moved in closer to hear her, the anxiety beginning to build once more.

"What is it?" he asked, gripping her hand.

"I've been keeping a secret from everyone, and it's eating me from the inside."

He shifted in his seat, mentally preparing himself for what was to come based on the way his mother was acting.

"Your father did not die from a suit malfunction when he was working on the exterior," she said flatly, staring up at the ceiling. Her eyes were red, though the tears had subsided.

Instead of questioning it, he sat in silence, waiting for more to come.

"He didn't want to continue anymore. I could see the pain behind his eyes. He didn't want to wait around to see me pass, and for him to be the one to leave you alone. So he went to work on the exterior wall, untethered himself, and let go. He just... let go. And I didn't stop him," she finished. She pulled her hand out of his grip and turned away the best she could.

He wasn't sure how to react, except the fact that the walls in the bedroom seemed to be constricting him. They seemed to be drawing nearer to him, the air thicker.

My hero. My father. Weak. And selfish for leaving her with the burden. And he didn't even bother to say goodbye?

They sat quietly for a moment longer, until the tension and pressure in the room was starting to choke him.

"It's not your fault," he rasped.

She turned her head and looked at him, light in her eyes. Her bottom lip quivered.

"You can't blame yourself for this. You've done everything you could." He fed her the words as if they were in an IV, pumping her with the nutrition she needed to survive. And he could tell that she held onto his words.

"You have grown into a very fine young man," she said, a hint of a smile tugging at her eyes. "I'm so proud of you, Arc," she whispered to him.

He watched her relax the muscles in her upper back and her arms as she leaned back, careful in the way she situated her body.

Thoughts were racing through his mind. Though

he felt he needed to comfort his Mom, she'd already put herself through so much. He still felt so much confusion.

Why did she keep this from me? It's not like I'm a little kid. She said this was a secret… but who else could know about this?

The conversation could go two ways. He could press her on the matter and open her wounds even further. Or he could accept the information he was hearing, digest it, and get back to her later with his questions. This wasn't the time for him to allow his emotions to overtake him.

"I met a girl," he said, looking forward at the wall behind her.

"Wha..what?" she asked, her voice higher than its usual tone.

He stifled a small laugh. "Dr. Lawlston has a new intern. She performed my check-in exam," he explained in a monotone.

I can't believe I'm telling her this…

And even though conversation was scarce on the ship, he usually didn't feel the need to share much of anything.

"What does she look like?" she asked, slightly amused at the turn the conversation was taking.

The mood was lighter, and it needed to be to keep their sanity.

He was curious why his Mom would ask about her looks first, of all things. Perhaps it was to see if she knew who he was talking about, if she'd seen this girl before. Arcturus couldn't imagine her intentions were superficial in any way.

"Like the brightest star in the Universe," he said, almost as if it was a song. He realized how ridiculous it sounded when it came out of his mouth.

Viona actually laughed out loud.

"She has yellow hair. And it's long, a lot longer than yours. Her face is perfect. Blue eyes, maybe? And she has these little marks on her face. Little brown spots that go over her nose and some of her cheekbones. And I love them. Every single one of them." He began to just speak, and he couldn't stop the words from freely flowing off his tongue.

"Freckles!"

"Huh?" he asked, turning to look at her, furrowing his brow.

"That's what they're called. The marks on her face are called freckles." She smiled.

It made sense he wouldn't know the word, it never came up in regular conversations they'd had over all the years—ranging from supernovas and gaseous balls of heat, to ice cream down on Earth in the heat of a southern summer in America. He contemplated the word.

"Well I like that word, too."

She laughed heartily from deep within her gut. "Well, will you get to see her again?" she pushed.

"I hope."

"I'm sure we could get something arranged with mission control."

"Mommm! No, let me deal with this. I'm almost thirty years old," he complained.

"All right, all right... " She smiled up at him. She reached up and placed the palm of her hand on his cheek.

He closed his eyes, embracing it this time.

"I think I'm going to get some rest... and you should too. I can feel us nearing the end, Arc... " She closed her eyes and hummed a single note for a moment.

"The end?" he asked quietly. He wasn't sure if she meant death, or what.

"Like you said, you're almost thirty. That means we're close to seeing what's outside our galaxy. Our whole reason for this mission, my whole reason for life itself." She smiled, turning from him to the window.

"Goodnight, Mom," he said, standing up and briefly checking the bandages he had fastened one more time.

"Night," she breathed.

CHAPTER FOUR

A Distant Kiss

Arcturus sat strapped into the pivoting chair as he listened to the monotonous humming of the electronics in the control room.

Killed himself...

He continued to replay the conversation he just had with Viona in his head, over and over again. As he rounded the curve in his mind where she told him his father untethered himself and let go, he dropped his chin to his chest. His eyes itched with drooping tiredness, and his energy felt as deflated as a shriveled up balloon.

With his chin resting upon the soft cotton material of the flight suit, he felt a chill wisp across the back of his shoulders, bracing his neck. He folded his arms over his chest and tightened them, rubbing the sides of his biceps for comfort.

Try to remember the last words you spoke to him.

He racked his own brain until it ached.

Was there any indication of a good bye that I couldn't see before? Anything?

If he had said some form of secret goodbye before he untethered himself, it wasn't verbal. Dex had been a reserved man who often kept to himself. Arcturus knew his father was only fond of the scientific truth, and left nothing to intuition or feeling. His dad's emotional responses to situations were next to nothing.

Arcturus' chestnut brown eyes glazed over, creating a shield against his outside stimulus, and he retreated back within himself before speaking softly,

"Well, I know the truth now... "

He reached up and grabbed hold of the temperature gauge he had suctioned on his forehead, where Diamandis told him to keep it, and peeled it off. A red beeping light started to flash on the left of the control panel as a quiet, high-pitched, flatlining tone sounded in his ears. He leaned forward and resisted against the buckle in his lap, as he scanned his finger over the blinking red light. He then activated the control panel to start up the QED connector. Beams of light shot up from the back of the control panel, fuzzing with white noise. Gray, white, and black pixels danced on the projected screen.

From Earth, the UniXplor mission control space station blurred into view on the screen. Instead of the exam room it had shown earlier, it was a large room with several rows of cubicles. The normally well-lit room was dimmed. It was nighttime, and the mission control crew normally went into sleep mode apart from the crew that got stuck on the night shift. UniX employees that helped coordinate and operate the complex elements of the *Homeland* mission filled the room. Though Arcturus grew up seeing the mission control research room, he more closely worked alongside the administration, including his physician and mentor, Lawlston.

He was aware that the people in this room were very important in helping conduct several of the experiments on the ship that advanced many areas in science and medicine, but he'd never spent much time getting to know the individuals behind the operations.

"Hey, Arc?" A large man with curly blonde hair and round, black-rimmed glasses stood up from one of the cubicles, two rows back.

"Yeah... hi!" He waved through the screen.

"Dr. Lawlston went home for the day... " he said nervously, as if his job never held enough importance to the point where he was able to converse with Arcturus.

"I'm actually looking for somebody else?" Arcturus spoke, speaking directly to the overweight man, who seemed to be the only one in the dark room with a desk lamp on.

"I can go get Dr. Zander if you need him?"

"Naw, not him." Arcturus shook his head.

"Who then?" he asked, startled.

"I'm looking for Diamandis." Her name even sounded beautiful forming on his lips.

"Diaman... the intern? I think she's gone as well. I can try to call her... "

"Please."

"Do you realize it's almost 2:30 am here?"

"No, I hadn't realized the sun set for the day and everyone was in bed," he said sarcastically, looking off to the side.

The man was nervous, and he wiped at what appeared to be sweat on his forehead.

Arcturus half rolled his eyes, then looked back at the screen. "I'm sorry... I didn't mean for it to sound like that. It's just very important that I speak to her. Is there any way you can contact her for me?" He slowed his voice down and spoke flatly, trying to redeem himself for being so rude.

"Uh... ye... ye..yes, sir," he stuttered.

Arcturus relaxed the tension in his face, closing his eyes for a moment before opening them to look up at the man once more.

Is this guy new? Or have I just never noticed him before...

He felt the nerves radiating off the man and through the screen.

Man, I'm an asshole. I should know this. Focus.

The man sat down at the desk and began moving his hand in the air, accessing the computer system in his glasses. Arcturus watched the top of his head moving back and forth in his cubicle, talking to somebody. He stood up into the monitor's view again.

"She wants t-t-to know that everything is okay?" he called up at Arcturus.

"No. I need to see her now."

"She wants to know why-why you took off y-your thermometer?" he asked.

"So I could get her attention."

The man stared at him just a moment longer than was comfortable.

"He says to get your attention. Yeah... hm... Yeah." He talked on his earpiece.

"She says she's coming in. She's on her way. C-can you sit tight?" he asked.

"Well I'm not really doing anything else, so yeah. Tell her I'll wait."

The man reached up and touched his earpiece, then looked back up at Arcturus.

"I'm g-going to get back to work here, so I'm going to turn oh-off the monitor. But when she gets here I'll have her connect w-with you from a different monitor, okay?"

He nodded.

The man leaned forward to turn off feed.

"Wait!" he shouted.

The man looked up at the screen, wide-eyed, as if he was worried at what would come next.

But Arcturus just smiled at him. "Thank you very much."

The guy gave a crooked smile and nodded at him. "My pleasure," he said quietly, and then he hit the button, disconnecting the camera feed.

He waited. He spun the chair around and pushed himself up and down the track. He turned back to the control panel and counted all the buttons on the board in front of him. Two hundred and twenty seven buttons. A lot more than the capsule had. He sighed from deep within his chest and leaned his head back to stare at the ceiling. Just when he was about to allow his eyelids to meet, a green button began to flash on the monitor. His attention closed in sharply on the button, and his stomach leaped up to his chest.

In the next moment, he was looking in on an exam room inside the mission control building.

"Arcturus?" He heard her voice, but couldn't see her.

"Yes! Yes, I'm here." He searched the screen.

Diamandis' head appeared on the side of his screen as she leaned into the camera.

She smiled instantly when she saw him. "Hey!" she said happily, her hands reaching up, getting close to the camera as she adjusted it onto herself. She was sitting up on an exam table, a counter behind her with medical tools lying out all over it, as if somebody had been sterilizing them all.

"Are you okay?" she asked softly, turning her head and looking into his eyes through the computer monitor.

71

"I am now..."

She looked different than the last time he saw her, probably because she wasn't in uniform. She was wearing a black cotton dress that puckered at her shoulders. It was a V-neck that scooped down between her breasts, and the skirt of the dress came to her knee as she sat up on the exam bed, her feet propped up on a chair.

"Did you seriously just take off the thermometer so I would come here?" she asked, her lips straight. There was a silence between them.

"I'm sorry. Actually I'm not sorry." He spoke quietly, barely parting his lips. He looked down, insecurity forcing him to question every motion and word.

She giggled. "Hmmm... You're a very curious man," she said, laughing again, and he saw her cheeks had turned a light shade of rose. He was pretty sure his own face had reciprocated.

"Why do you think that?" he asked, interested in what she had to say, but mostly just wanting to hear her voice.

"We've only just met. I'm sure you could have called in anybody to talk to." She said.

"I don't want to talk to just anybody. In fact, I

barely like talking at all."

"It's nearly 3am here, you know..." she started slowly, and then continued before he could speak. "Not that I don't want to talk to you. I really do. It's just I'm usually in bed at this time, and I worked a really long shift today," she finished.

The only thing he heard was that she said she really wanted to talk to him.

"I just... I had to see you again, Dia. Please... just stay with me a while?" He asked, looking down at his bare feet, the ankle straps tightly around them.

"I won't go anywhere," she smiled. "So what do you want to talk about?" she asked, propping her chin up with her fists, her elbows resting on her knees.

"Are you with somebody?" he asked.

"No, I'm the only one in the room. For goodness sake, Arc, I told you it was 3am."

"No. I meant uhh... how do you say it? Do you have an intimate companion?" he asked, a little more confident this time.

She moved her head back and forth slowly, replying no. "Do you?" she asked, a small hint of a smirk on her lips.

"You have a sense of humor," he said slyly, appreciating it. Clearly his pick of companions on the ship were zero. "But yeah, you know... I get around." He winked at her.

Was that creepy? Those cultural movies are stupid. The back of his neck warmed.

He watched Diamandis as she laughed heartily. She lifted her head back up to look at him, her eyes squinting at the edges.

"You want to know something?" she asked him, the creases from her eyes by her temples subsiding.

"Yeah?" he asked.

"I've been learning about you since I was a little girl. I know so much about you, Arc. Just like everybody else. But I don't know *you*. It feels so surreal that you, of all people, would call me at 2:30am, just because you want to hear my voice. Why me?"

He watched her while she spoke. He pressed his palm against the earpiece so he could hear her better.

"Because when I see you on the other side of the screen, I'm taken somewhere else. I'm always here on this ship, Dia. It's my whole world. You may think I'm free because I am in interstellar space, and it's grand and beautiful and infinite. But it's a prison. A prison that I can never leave... When I saw you earlier, it's as if nothing else existed. And I could see the sunlight on your face. I've been traveling through deep space since I was born. It's been twenty nine years, you know that. And I've never seen something so bright... so beautiful," he finished. When he looked up at her through the screen, he saw that her face was grave. Her lips were puckered, and she sniffled. He watched as she lifted her hand and wiped at her eyes, shaking her head a moment and turning away.

"Sorry," she said quickly, smiling at him with her teeth.

"Did I upset you?" he asked, alarmed, leaning in to the screen.

"No! No... " she said softly. "It's just... nobody's ever said something so raw to me before... and I... thank you." She brushed at her eyes once more.

He nodded as she shifted in her seat. She turned her head and then pulled her long, wavy blond hair back into a ponytail, tying it up with the hair tie she wore around her wrist.

"Are you sure you want to get to know me when... well... " She trailed off.

He watched her nervous antics, the way she kept slicking the sides of her ponytail.

"Go on. I can take it," he said, hoping he could.

"Well, what if we never meet in person? You're

not supposed to come home until... "

Arcturus was quiet for a moment. He looked away from the screen, over to the vaulted door that led to the asteroid mining capsule. Deflation began to draw nearer for a moment, but he decided to let it pass because he couldn't bear to waste the time while he was talking to her.

"One can hope, right?" he asked, looking back at her.

"Yes," she answered truthfully, wistfully.

"I was *hoping* you'd say that," he said, emphasizing the word 'hope'. She laughed.

There was a moment of silence.

"So how is Viona—your Mom I mean?" she asked, changing the subject. "Lawlston said she suffered a bad fall."

"Yeah, she's all right." He looked behind him as if to signify where she was at in the ship in reference to him. "She's resting. She hurt her shoulder pretty badly," he finished, snapping his head back to the screen.

"I'm sorry," she answered, looking to the side.

"It gets harder for her every day, you know."

She nodded, biting her bottom lip.

"Can I share something with you?" he asked.

"Of course," she whispered to him. She hopped off the exam table and sat in the chair she previously had her feet on. She wheeled up close to the camera, so that all he could see was everything above her shoulders.

"Nobody else knows this," he warned her.

She nodded.

"My Mom shared with me today... that... that my dad killed himself." He watched her reaction carefully.

Diamandis' eyes widened, and her hand shot up to cover her mouth. Furrowing her brow, she shook her head back and forth.

"No. It was a flight suit malfunction when he was doing the—"

"No. That's what everyone thinks. But we were here. And she says he told her he couldn't take it anymore. She decided to tell me because she said she couldn't carry the burden of it any longer."

"Oh, Arc... I'm so, SO sorry."

He watched her eyebrows crinkle as a pained sadness consumed her eyes. Part of the weight on Arcturus' chest lifted as he observed her reaction to his news.

This is the first time she's hearing this. He let out

a deep breath he'd held onto, trying to conceal his sense of relief.

At least Mom was telling the truth when she told me she was the only one who knew.

His mother was trying to protect him, but there was a part of him that knew it was possible he was the only one who didn't know the truth about his father's death.

"If there's anything I can do... " She lifted her chin to look at him.

He searched her eyes, from one to the other. "Naw, s'okay. We all die. I just wish he hadn't been so selfish, to leave my Mom with so many burdens. I could tell how heartbroken she was when she told me, you know?" He reached back and rubbed the back of his neck.

"Arc... your father was a great man. He took care of the two of you for so many years. He taught you the skills you needed to take care of your mother and to run the ship yourself."

He started to space out as she spoke, his mind wandering from the conversation as his eyes glazed over. "It's okay. You don't have to... say those things. Really."

Although he was relieved that Viona was telling

the truth, and he understood Dex's motives, he still needed time to let it sink in.

I deserve to be mad at him. He thought. *Though Dia's just trying to comfort me.*

When he brought his attention back to the conversation, Diamandis was still talking.

"And although I didn't know him as well as you did, I feel like he never would have left Viona if he felt like she couldn't handle it. She's a very strong woman. My mom has told me stories about her, and how inspiring she was, going around giving speeches at different places about the mission... "

He listened to her voice come through the QED.

She reached up and brushed away a strand of hair that didn't make it into her ponytail.

At least she changed the subject to Viona. I can deal with that.

"Yeah... " he trailed off. He tried to pat down his hair that was standing up straight from the lack of gravity as it so often did, forming a sort of afro from his thick black curls.

"Thank you," he said quietly and she nodded, watching him pat his hair.

"It'll be all right," she said with a smile, and it was his turn to nod.

"So you know a lot of details about my life then, huh?" he asked.

"Well I don't mean to freak you out or anything..."

"No, it's okay! It's interesting to me actually," he replied quickly.

"You know many details about *Homeland* are kept very private." Her voice was soft spoken. "...But you're a celebrity, Arc. I hope you know that, at least." She smiled.

He scrunched up his nose. "No idea why." He was cynical.

"No idea why?" She mocked. "You're the only human who was ever born in outer space! That's unreal." She paused a moment and looked straight through him. "You just wanted to hear that again... C'mon! You have to know how popular you are here on the ground."

"It's normal for me," he answered, shrugging his shoulders. "My mom has shared a lot of things with me about Earth and the culture of the United States, but whenever I watch or learn about your everyday life, I feel as though time is frozen and I'm getting a delay of the truth or something. I'll never really know what it's like to live on Earth, will I?" he asked her.

She turned her head in thought. "That's an interesting perspective," she said. "It's like... we all long to know what it's like to be you, and you long to know what it's like to be on Earth. Can we ever achieve the satisfaction we seek, you know?" she asked.

"That's exactly what I was going for." he said, just above a whisper. "I think about that all the time. You know I've got a lot of time with my own thoughts."

They laughed in unison.

"So since you know a lot about me, it's my turn to find out about you," he continued.

She nodded, straightening her spine.

"Do you have any siblings?"

"Only child. Like you," she smiled.

He nodded. "How old are you?"

"You must never ask a woman her age," she smirked.

"Why not?" he asked. He genuinely didn't understand.

She laughed out loud. "It's just something people say, because woman like to conceal their age. I was teasing. I'm twenty-three," she finished.

"Holy crap, I'm six years older than you?"

She laughed, closing her eyes a moment and opening them back up to look at him. "I've always been mature for my age."

"Are you in school?" he asked.

"I have one more year left. Which is why I'm interning. I'm going into the medical field. I was selected out of thousands of applicants to follow Dr. Lawlston. I have a certain love for space medicine."

Arcturus loved to watch her talk: the way her she scrunched her nose when she laughed, and how her freckled cheekbones grew rosy when he spoke back to her.

"I'm finding I'm getting a lot more than I expected from it." She smiled at him, rosy cheeks once more.

Does she mean because of me? He swallowed the saliva in his mouth, nervous that it'd made too loud of a gulp.

She rubbed her eyes with the back of her fist, covering her mouth as she yawned. He returned her yawn.

"Yawning's contagious," he said, open-mouthed. "I know you're tired, but I don't want to let you go. I'm happy when I see you, Dia. I want to know more about you," he said nervously, afraid of rejection even though she never gave him any signs of being close to that.

"You don't have anything to worry about. I'm drawn to you," she said, and the corner of her lips curved upward.

At the sound of her words, his heart began to race. His knees were shaky, and he was glad to be sitting down.

"And we've got a lot of time. Are you getting excited about your distance?" she asked, bringing their conversation back to the mission.

"It's the whole reason I'm alive, right?" he asked, then continued. "My mom is getting weaker by the day, but she's also more excited than ever that the end is near. I'm so happy she'll be here to see it. And once we've collected all the data we need and have seen firsthand what's outside our galaxy, we'll be able to turn around and head back home."

"And you'll be everyone's hero," she smiled.

"I'm not so worried about that as much as the long journey that still lies ahead."

Her face relaxed again, saddened. "Yeah... " she said quietly. "But I believe in you, Arc. I know you can do it. You have it in your blood."

He looked into her eyes. They were blue. Crystal

clear, blue eyes. He moved toward the screen, as if he was in the same room and could touch her cheek.

"I wish... " he trailed off. "Diamandis... I'd really like to kiss you." His voice was just above a whisper.

She looked at him first, then slowly reached up her index and middle finger together on her lips.

"Put your fingers like this," she whispered, and she trailed her fingers perpendicularly down her lips as she closed her long, thick lashes. Her hand trailed down to her neck. With her lips slightly parted, she opened her eyes back up to look at him. He watched her, an intense ball of rising energy swirling in his gut and moving up through him and out his fingertips, tingling his lips. Her stare was misty, icy, beautiful, and he couldn't keep his eyes off her.

CHAPTER FIVE

Unfair

"Man... " Arcturus sighed, reliving the conversation he just had with Diamandis. He pictured her lips as she ran her fingers down them for him. He felt a tightening in his gut, and he turned from the control panel. He grabbed a water pouch from one of the cabinets before making his way for the sleep rooms.

He clenched his teeth down on the plastic, crinkling the straw of the pouch and squeezed it. A bubble of liquid emerged through the top, and he stretched his neck out. He puckered his lips and sucked up the bubble, swallowing with a huge gulp.

The water soothed his throat as it went down.

He slid the door open and glanced over at his bed. Viona lay on her side with her back to him. He saw her body rising and falling with natural REM sleep breathing. With the paragravity hardware in their sleeping rooms, it was hard to move her somewhere far with her injury. He knew the medication they instructed him to give her was going to knock her out for a while.

He tiptoed his way back out the door into the hall, gaining access to his parent's room. He closed the doors shut behind him and looked around, the room almost an identical image to his own. The walls and floors were silver. Their beds were off to the left, two twin mattress pads that his parents had pushed together to make one bigger bed.

When he was little, he would slide open that door between their rooms and crawl up into bed with them. It was the warmest and safest place he knew. It was home. Being in his parent's room was a privilege. There was something mystical and altogether magical about it, like the feeling a child has when they see presents under their tree on Christmas morning.

Arcturus' eyes glazed over as he remembered the time he learned about Santa Claus.

Quite often people would write letters to Dex, Viona, and Arcturus. There was an entire team back in mission control that received and went through all the fan mail, mailing back a generic reply with a photo of *Homeland.*

One time Arcturus got a letter from a child his age that talked about Santa Claus and decorating a Christmas tree for their home. He'd seen movies with Santa in them, but it just never occurred to him that this wasn't something they ever participated in, though it was important to learn the traditions of the culture he was supposedly from.

"Momma? How come Santa won't visit me? What 'bout other kids in space?" He remembered asking her after he learned about these customs most American children knew.

"It's hard for reindeer to go out of Earth?" he persisted.

Viona told him that although it was fun to play, Santa Claus wasn't a real person. She explained to him that it was fun and magical to make up things, but that it was important to also know the truth.

Arcturus moseyed over to his parents' bed and sat down on the edge.

It was then that I realized I was the only kid in space.

He reached up and ran his hand through his

hair, stopping at the back of his neck and holding it there as he looked down at the ground, then back at the pillows.

Man it'd be nice to just lay down here and rest...

And though his eyes itched with exhaustion, it wasn't going to happen.

He couldn't shake the image of those sparkling, vibrant, blue eyes staring back at him. And the distance of their ship. They were so close.

So close!

So close to reaching their goal of getting a spacecraft outside of the Milky Way Galaxy. Their ship had already gone the farthest any man had ever gone. They would have direct access to discover exactly what was out there beside themselves, whether it be a new resource or another form of mankind.

This mission has always been something I've had to do. Something out of my control. I was born to collect information and bring it back.

He rested his elbows on his knees with his forehead in his hands. He looked at the ground.

Maybe there is a chance for me. To find what they want and head back to Earth, towards... towards...

Towards something he never thought he'd be

able to experience in his lifetime. To have a woman to hold, somebody to hold him. Somebody other than his parents.

And then it hit him like a freight train slamming straight into his chest. He exhaled and his throat tightened, making it harder for him to breathe.

"Even if I make it back to Earth... " He breathed in, the air thicker than ever, his lungs constricted. He needed to reach up and wrap his hands around his throat.

"... I'll be an old man. My youth will be gone." Speaking the words aloud made them real. Tension built in every bit of his body. He balled up a fist, squeezing his hand together so hard that his knuckles turned white. As he released the anger, he brought his fist sideways and slammed it into the side of *Homeland.*

"Dammit!" he yelled, knowing that the soundproof barrier between rooms kept his mother from waking. He felt nothing at first, and then the blood rushed to his knuckles. They pulsated. Ached. Allowing his weight to fall into the wall, he leaned on it as if all his energy had been released through the punch.

"Dammit... " It came out as only a whisper this

time. Hot tears seeped out of the crease in his eyes and trailed down the side of his temple, disappearing into his hairline. It was in that moment that he realized just how unfair his life had been, and how unfair it would be from that point until his death.

Exhale.

Inhale. Sweat began to form at his brow as heat rose on the back of his neck. Trembling muscles in his biceps pulled him up, and his chin rose above the steel bar in the doorframe of the left wing of the ship.

He spent a lot of his time in the left wing, an attachment to the sleep modules, which held training and exercise equipment. Lifting weights and conditioning his body became a favorite pastime, providing a way he could be on his own with his thoughts, without his parents questioning his well-being. It was a common fact that the musculoskeletal system continuously deteriorated in interstellar space. The fact that they had paragravity hardware in certain parts of the ship helped curb this fate, though it was important that he continued to condition his body to its limits.

He let his arms straighten, legs dangling down

under the steel bar, knees bent.

The edge of the galaxy was drawing nearer, and although they'd waited their whole lives for this moment, he welcomed this distraction. He had a whole team of people back at mission control working on their distance and statistics. The only thing was, they were monitoring *Homeland* in uncharted territory, and even though they were present, there wasn't much mission control could do for them besides give their input and expertise. It's not as if they could swoop on in or send an emergency vehicle to save them in a time of need.

Arcturus stripped off his clothes, wearing just his black, form fitting boxer briefs. As he continued to do pull-ups on the bar, every defined muscle in his body shook and tightened as he worked it. A warm sweat materialized on his skin, pale from having never been touched by the sun.

He jumped down off the pull-up bar and shook his hands, gaining color back after his tight grip around the bar. After he walked over to the wall and pulled out a drawer, he fetched a hand towel to wipe his face and the back of his neck, retrieving a silver pouch of water and helping himself to it.

As he gulped down the water, he walked over to

the rectangular window that showed a view of the exterior of the ship. Using his hand, he stabilized himself on the bench in front of the window, leaning in to catch a glimpse. *Homeland* was moving so fast it was hard to see anything but blurs of light as they passed.

Tension hung in the air as they were drawing nearer to their destination, and Arcturus felt it not only around *Homeland*, but also through the screen to mission control. He'd spent his whole life in this ship, and he couldn't help but feel a distance from the rest, more so than the physical one that stood between them.

"Errgg... " he moaned and rubbed at his goopy eyes as he reached his arm up over his head, resting his forehead on his bent arm. After a long, imaginary hitting of the snooze button, he turned over on the bed and rolled towards the edge. He sat up, unzipped the white flight suit, and peeled the moistened fabric off his shoulders and back. He allowed the fabric to hang at his hips, leaving the pants on.

After he crossed the room, groggy, Arcturus bumped into the wall before he turned his body sideways to slip into the bathroom. He didn't need to use the ankle straps or lap bar provided on the toilet because he was in the section of *Homeland* that used artificial gravity. He grabbed the vacuum tube, attached the male funnel to it, and relieved himself. The vacuum tube would send his urine into a tank that processed it and extracted the impurities to re-condense it back into water.

When finished, he made sure to remove the male attachment and put his mother's back on. Her voice echoed in his mind all the complaints, equivalent to complaining that he didn't put the seat down.

After his urine dispensed into the blackened oblivion, he came back into the sleep pod and yanked out one of the drawers from the wall, retrieving two silver pouches. Marked with a barcode, the pouches read the familiar word, "Breakfast".

He bit open one of the straws and sucked the tasteless nutrients that kept his stomach from aching and growling. The light turned green as he scanned his hand over the pad to enter into his own sleep room, where Viona was sleeping.

When he saw her body absent from the bed, he choked on the gel he was swallowing, coughing to clear his throat. He looked around in haste, confirming she was nowhere in the room. Making his way through the ship, he searched everywhere he went. He entered into zero gravity, and used his arms and legs as propulsion to swim through the tunnel to the great room.

"Mommm!"

No answer. He slid open the door to the control room. The monitor was on, and she was sitting in front of it, talking to the control center.

"Mom!" Arcturus shouted again, holding himself in the doorframe. Strapped to the swivel chair, she moved the whole chair rather than her head so she didn't stretch her shoulder.

"Hey, Sweetie!" she said happily, yet slowly, because she was still taking pain medicine.

He stood staring, his lips thin.

"What's the matter?" she asked, officers from mission control standing behind her on the screen.

"You can't do that! Disappear after what you just told me yesterday!" he shouted, staring at her.

"Arc, there's a time and place for this—"

"Viona, it looks like you need to get back to tending to—"

"No, Leo, it's all right I'll take—"

From the doorway, Arcturus interjected, "No—Leo, you stay, whoever you are. I can go. It's okay."

He began to spin around.

"Arc!" Her voice was stern.

He looked at her with a raised eyebrow.

"You were sleeping. I didn't want to wake you up, you haven't slept fourteen hours in a very long time. Your body needed it."

"Fourteen hours! I slept fourteen hours?"

She nodded, a look of concern on her face. "Have you looked outside since you've awakened?"

He shook his head. He looked behind him, through the great room to the hallway he rushed through in haste before. He hadn't even glanced outside when he was looking for his Mom.

"We've entered into clouds of dust," she whispered.

"We're almost...?"

She nodded. She patted for him to come sit next to her. He let go of the doorframe and pushed off towards her, pulling a seat out from under the counter. Unfolding the chair and placing it on the track, he sat down and buckled himself in. He reached his hand out and held out the pouch to her.

"I brought you breakfast."

"More like dinner," she teased.

"You could have woken me, you know," he replied through gritted teeth, nodding at her wrapped shoulder.

"It's my shoulder that's hurt, Arc, not my legs. Besides, it feels better with no gravity because the pressure is off it," she reasoned with him.

He looked up at mission control.

"I apologize for the interruption... "

"Arc, this is Leo. He's taking over as head for his father, Zander, who's retired. We are lucky to have him."

She sounds so rehearsed. Does this guy even know anything about the mission? ... I've got more important things to worry about.

"Great. Have we run any of the elements in our exterior yet?" He chose to ignore the introduction, which didn't seem to sit well with Viona.

"You could at least welcome him to the—"

Leo cut her off, clearly not concerned with an introduction either. "We were just checking the levels from outside the craft. We've never gotten these high levels of radiation before, and even though *Homeland* has that half an inch of lead around it, we're worried how much it can withstand before you guys are exposed to dangerous levels. It might have to do with the coordinates we entered when doing the jump." He looked down at a clipboard.

"You did a jump? Serious?" Arcturus shot his head over to Viona. "Mom. Without me? This is ridic—"

"You need to calm down, Arc. You need to trust that things are going to happen without you sometimes."

"In time, nothing will happen without me." He crossed his arms over his chest, feeling a familiar heat on the back of his neck, instantly regretting it. A silence pulled the room thin between them.

Leo cut in, "We understand you need all the practice you can get so you're conditioned for when you are conducting jumps on your own, but the initial goal is still in our hands. So you need to cooperate."

Arcturus brought his attention back to the screen and narrowed his eyes.

Who does this guy think he is?

Before he could think any further, Lawlston spoke up behind Leo.

"We're worried about the temperature drop you will be facing, and if it will effect the interior and how you guys feel. Is the air any different?"

Arcturus took in a deep breath. "Actually, I woke up kind of hot. Sweating, even." He looked down and realized for the first time since he entered the room that he was shirtless. He was so heated from disorientation and out of the loop from sleeping so long, that he forgot he took off the top half of his flight suit.

The three men in the view of the camera gave each other looks, and the unnamed man left the fore screen and went into a cubicle behind them.

"All right, I'm going to switch feed to one of the exam rooms where Lawlston is waiting so he can instruct you, Arc, on how to change your Mom's bandages without damaging her bones further, even if you don't mean to. And I'm going to send through this scaling chart for several experiments we'll need you to conduct while you're in transitioning phase to the outskirts of the galaxy—if you can see through all that dust and debris."

Arcturus nodded, and although Leo's words were quick, he soaked it all in like a sponge.

"Arcturus, you are going to need to do these on your own, because Viona—" He turned and spoke directly to her.

"You need to relax a bit. It's okay if you watch Arc, but you need to take it easy. Don't push yourself for a change, especially if you want to see what you gave your life for."

Viona didn't say a word, but pursed her lips and looked over at her son.

"It'll be all right." He smiled, knowing how angry it made her when somebody told her she wasn't physically capable of doing something.

"All right, Leo. Transfer us." He reached down and grabbed his flight suit, pulling it up over his shoulders, though he left the front unzipped as the screen went blank a moment, losing feed during the transfer to Lawlston's room.

The screen flashed again, and Dr. Lawlston appeared in the exam room.

Arcturus looked past Lawlston to the exam table to his left, the same exam table Diamandis sat on when she spoke to him last night. He noticed the tools that had been on the counter weren't there anymore. Warmth fogged up his chest as he thought of the time they spent together.

"Right?" Viona asked him, bringing his mind back to the room.

"Uh, huh?" he asked, looking from his Mom to Lawlston.

"Arc, if you're going to do this right, you have to pay attention!" she scolded.

"What's with the new guy?" he asked Lawlston, avoiding his mother's gaze.

"He's not new, Arc. He's been working with the team for years."

"Yeah, but why is he all high and mighty now?"

"I told you his father retired." Viona answered before Lawlston could. "He died."

"Pancreatic cancer." Lawlston finished. "Yes, Leo has lost his father, just like you. Any other questions?"

He didn't lose his father exactly like I did...

Arcturus thought bitterly as he took a moment to breathe.

"Yeah, how will my Mom's injuries affect her leaving the galaxy?" he asked.

"Well... It's hard to say. We're just going to have you keep a close eye. Just take care of each other the way you always have. I can prescribe a pain medication I hoped we would never have to use, but it could make her very drowsy and it may just knock her out," he explained, turning to document something on the touch screen pad that was sitting flat on the counter, almost transparent.

Arcturus looked over at Viona, his frail mother's face deflating before him. She looked beat, the bags under her eyes more prominent than ever.

"Hey, Lawlston. Let's just go over the stuff about changing her bandages, okay? Then I can put you on standby."

"We'll be here Arc. We've called in the whole team so we can monitor progress." He stopped a moment and walked up to the camera.

"Now before we get started... need I ask if you guys are excited?"

His lips parted into a grin.

CHAPTER SIX

Who Leads,
Who Follows

Arcturus finished zipping up a fresh, navy blue jumpsuit and walked over to the window above his bed. He left his father's white suit crumpled on the floor in front of the steel drawers on the wall. Lawlston and Viona were back in the control room. He left them alone to talk about her health and her emotional expectations about going into the end of their mission.

He squinted as he peered out the rectangular frame, and wasn't able to see anything but darkness. They were traveling through such thick dust and debris that the familiar streams of light and barreling asteroids were nowhere in sight. No signs of discomfort or turbulence bothered the ship, and they could account that to the great design and mechanical engineering of *Homeland.* If they did have a run in with debris, it was able to roll up and over the top of the spacecraft, allowing it to move through deep space unnoticed and unharmed.

He leaned over and grabbed the tablet on his bed. He swiped it open and pulled up the scaling chart Leo sent over for him to complete. The only reason for scaling was due to the fact that nobody knew what they were facing.

"Unmapped territory... " he whispered. A smirk tugged at the side of his lips. It sounded adventurous. The only problem was UniX mission control wasn't sure if the ship could withstand the pressure, materials, or elements that made up the area outside the galaxy, because well, there would probably be less of everything. They had no idea how their equipment would react.

"Hmph." He stretched his neck from side to side. *All I can do is what I was trained to do.*

He let out a long, drawn out breath of air and rose to collect the supplies he needed to begin sampling.

The door slid open and Viona entered. She shuffled slowly, her silver hair down her back. She usually wore it up.

Arcturus stopped and straightened himself to look at her.

"You're not going to take that medicine, are you?" He already knew the answer.

"My child... " She leaned her head against the doorframe as if gravity was a burden, her eyes watery.

"I've had enough medicine... " She closed her eyes for a moment.

He watched her closely. "You can't just give up like that. I know you," he challenged.

"I've waited my whole life to experience this. And I did not come this far to sleep through it." Her voice crescendoed. No matter what she'd have to go through, she would hold onto her passion for seeing to the end of the galaxy. It was evident.

He put his hands up as if she'd caught him red handed. "Okay. Nobody's stopping you." He half smiled. "But will you at least lay down and take a nap? I'm going to get started on this ridiculous list of shit that I have to take care of, " he started.

"Hey, you watch your mouth!" she corrected him. "Take that 'shit' seriously, Arc. It's very important to document."

Her tone was light. The smile on her lips told him that she wasn't serious.

"I know... I know... " He smiled and shook his head back and forth. "Go get some rest. I promise I'll wake you if anything exciting happens. Though right now we're just in the black. I imagine we're passing through dust clouds of some sort. Hopefully we'll be out of this storm soon. Have you noticed the temperature dropped?" He looked down at the chart.

"I most certainly have. I'm actually wearing two flight suits," she said, looking down at her thick, bulging black uniform.

"You mean to tell me you're even smaller than the way you look now, under two layers of suit?" he asked the rhetorical question, raising his eyebrow at her.

"All right, I'm getting out of here before you pick on me some more. Love you, son." She swatted her hand at him and started to cross the room, heading for her own bed.

"I feel like we got off on the wrong foot." Leo sat at a desk, his face closer to the camera than Arcturus would have preferred.

He stationed the tablet inside a mechanical arm on the wall, and sat down on the edge of the bed as he connected with mission control. "What does that even mean?" he asked, pushing himself back from the edge of his bed, leaning his back against the wall.

"Our first meeting didn't go so well."

"Aye."

Arcturus stared at Leo's blond, spiky hair. Though his hair was blond like Diamandis', it wasn't the same warm, golden yellow that hers was. His was pasted up, as if he'd used an entire bottle of hair gel.

"I just felt like I haven't seen you my entire life, not even around the station, and then all the sudden you're the Head Administrator."

Leo clicked a pen open and closed on his desk. Repetitively.

"Why do I need to prove my credentials to you?" he spat.

Arcturus laughed under his breath. "You don't."

"I know you better than you know yourself," Leo said.

"Is that so?" Arcturus narrowed his eyes.

"I've known you my whole life." Leo looked down from the monitor.

The tone in his voice made Arcturus perk his ears. He hadn't even given this guy a chance. Maybe he wasn't half bad. They were the same age, maybe they could be on the same side, if there were even sides. Regardless, he was getting very irritated with everyone telling him how they knew him more than he knew himself. They didn't know anything he'd been through, or was presently going through.

"I've been hearing that a lot lately," he spoke back in a hushed tone.

"I remember like it was yesterday... My father came home from work one day, where he spent countless hours. More hours than he ever spent with my Mom and me..."

"Where is this going?" Arcturus interrupted.

Leo stared back up at him with his snake eyes.

"He came home from work one day with a brand new, first edition flight suit that our hero Arcturus wore. I was so happy."

"That makes me slightly uncomfortable." Arcturus smiled.

"You can't begin to understand the effect you've had on our society. I grew up next to you, Arc. I was born the same year as you. I had a toy helmet, and vanity toy *Homeland*. It was as if after Viona and Dex announced their pregnancy, a baby boom hit the nation."

"Baby boom?"

"A significant amount of people had children. I was one of those babies," Leo finished.

"Can you explain to me how any of this is my

fault?" Arcturus asked earnestly, all joking aside.

"It's not. But it's not my fault either. And in this respect we should understand each other."

"What's there to understand? You're an asshole." It slipped. But Arcturus owned it.

Leo rolled his eyes, backing up from the screen in a rolling chair. "If that's the way you want to play, then I can play." His voice was low, chilling. "Finish what you've been instructed to do. That is all."

Before Arcturus could muster another word, Leo reached forward and cut the feed.

It was the cessation of the constant humming moan of the generator turning off that woke him in the night. Arcturus turned over onto his side and stared out the window cut out at eye level above his bed. He saw nothing but black. It was always night here.

He reached up and rubbed his tired, crusty eyes with the back of his fist. He closed his eyelids.

Just a moment longer...

"Arc!... "

He thought he heard somebody calling him from the other side of a long, far away tunnel.

"Arc!"

The voice was buried behind clouds of fog. It was an airy, woman's voice.

"Heyyy!" Urgency in her voice this time. And it was closer. He quietly groaned, peeling his eyes open. He had to blink twice before the outline of his mother's body came into view.

"Wake up! Can you not hear that the generator went out?" Viona called at Arcturus from the other side of the room.

He sighed and lifted his heavy head up. "I thought I sanctioned a surplus last time," he whined, rubbing his eyes once more.

"It has nothing to do with the fuel. Get up. Now!" she answered, matter-of-factly, and she left no room for a rebuttal.

He tore his eyes away from the black outside his window, and rolled over, off the small, flat bed underneath the window.

"You know I wouldn't nag if it wasn't a matter of life or death." Viona crossed her arms over her chest.

"Everything's a matter of life or death," he complained.

I'll get to the asteroid mining capsule to refuel in just a second... right after I... I...

Arcturus shot up in the bed.

"There aren't any gray clouds or debris out there." He stated the obvious, looking at the window once again. "Did you do another jump while I was sleeping?" he shouted at her.

She shook her head no.

"This must be it?" he asked in disbelief, wrestling his blankets off as he got out of bed. He breathed heavily, and looked outside once more.

Black. Not that it wasn't black before, but this was foggy, with debris passing by them, the same color as the backdrop it lay in. As he looked, deep in the distance he thought he spotted a speck of something orange; something burning. He strained his eyes, staring in that direction.

Then, he shut his eyes tight and opened them again as if it would clear his vision.

What the... is it an illusion? Am I dreaming?

As they drew closer to the light, he confirmed that his eyes were really seeing what he thought they were.

"Whaa..?" He spoke aloud, staring one second longer, before he turned to her. "Mom!"

Viona smiled. "Help—help me to the AGC," she said quickly, serious.

He hurried to her side and allowed her to use him as a crutch in aiding her to the AGC.

"We need to get to the control room, and we need to grab our external flight suits."

She shook her head back and forth, refusing.

He stopped and turned to face her. "Mom! We need to get to the control room, like we planned in protocol!"

"I'll go, I'll go. Just don't waste time getting my suit," she said quietly.

"Why?" he demanded.

"Because we both know I'm not going to need it," she said sternly. "I'm weak, Arc. I've had enough. I'm done. I know I'm not going to make it, and so it's not worth wasting our time to go and fetch my suit. Now we need to go. Now. Please, help me."

He hesitated for just a moment, watching Viona and realizing defeat. He bent down under her arm and scooped up her legs, holding her as if she were a child, crumpled in his arms. She moaned from the pain in her shoulder as he lifted her. He carried her through the doorframe to the AGC, where he used the strength in his legs to carry her.

"Can you stand? Just for a second, then I'll re-lease the air pressure."

She nodded her head and he very carefully set her on the floor, standing shakily on her feet, hunched over by his side. He ran back out of the defusing room and into his sleep room, fetching the case that held his external flight suit, oxygen, and helmet with one hand.

When he made it back, he slammed his hand down on the circular red button and defused the paragravity hardware, lifting them from their feet. He then opened the door and they floated out into the long corridor, windows on all sides. Viona followed behind him and swam with one arm. His heart was pounding, adrenaline keeping him going. Viona stopped behind him, reaching out quickly and grabbing the sleeve of his suit, just above his elbow. He turned to look at her, and realized his mother's face had frozen, stunned as she stared out the large windows. He followed her eyes out to the exterior.

The energy in his limbs, the feeling in his heart was immense. They were standing on the edge of the galaxy, a place where no human had stood before. A clear line where the dust, smoke, and debris had contained itself and followed the curve. And looking ahead, he saw what he thought to be Andromeda, the closest galaxy to our own. As he expanded his focus and looked around, he absorbed the fact that the entire environment was peppered here and there with lots of galaxies apart from their own that they just left. Because of telescopes back on Earth, they'd known there were billions of galaxies out there. But to actually see it. To actually stand in the presence of countless other galaxies. Other possibilities.

It was something no man had ever witnessed before.

It was beautiful.

CHAPTER SEVEN

The Funeral

His eyes crossed following a water bubble as it wiggled by his line of sight. He focused past the droplet. Viona curled up in a ball, glancing sideways out into the darkness of the graphene glass corridor. Her features petrified as tears emerged from the ducts in her eyes, each one forming another water bubble in the air.

I need to cut progression.

"Mom. Hold... hold on. I'll be right back, okay?"

He turned from the hallway and headed towards the control room. The ship continued to run on autopilot, and he needed to stop it and keep the ship in one place until they planned their next move.

He pushed off the wall and paddled over to the opposite wall of the control room. As he reached the panel and placed his hands down upon the keys, a surge of nerves prickled up his arms.

He racked his brain for the numbers he needed to input into the motherboard, and slammed the palm of his hand down on a large knob. Even inputting just one number wrong could break the chain of commands he intended for *Homeland*. And he didn't need any more distractions as he was preparing to say goodbye to his mother, especially if he was going to leave the ship entirely. He held his breath a moment. The humming of the generators powered down, gargling, followed by a shrilling alarm.

"Override! Override!" The sound was splitting in his eardrums.

This had never happened before.

Arcturus squeezed his eyes shut and inhaled deeply from his gut. "Let go... of the nerves. You can do this." His voice relaxed, and after he reiterated several more numbers, the alarm hushed.

With the alarm muffled, though not completely turned off, he sent in some key commands to mission control, so they knew what was going on.

He turned, eyeing his exterior suit in its case floating around the room.

Since he was in such a haste to stop *Homeland*, he hadn't realized that he let go of the case, allowing it to float freely. He was going to need that suit later.

After finishing everything practical he learned to do since he was born, he swam over to the door-frame once more to join up with his mother in front of the large windows.

Galaxies spiraled on forever, hues of orange, red, blue, green, and yellow.

Though telescopes and satellites had taken photos of the expectations of the outside of our galaxy, nothing could prepare them for this moment.

And though it was a sight to see for Arcturus, he simply couldn't imagine the feelings that were running through Viona's body.

"Mom?" He inched closer and closer to her.

She opened her lips to speak, though no words escaped her mouth.

Arcturus moved closer and put his arm around her, pulling her close. "Are you... all right?"

Once the baby she held in her arms, her son now towered over her petite and fragile body. She curled her knees up to her chest once more.

"I'm... I can't... " She tried to form words. "The possibilities." She spoke, her voice more high pitched than normal. Her lips parted into a smile, and he searched both of her eyes as they sparkled.

It's going to be all right. Everything is going to be all right.

He told himself, though this time believed it would be. And he understood. Looking out at the Universe from outside of the Milky Way, he understood why his mother chose to give her life for this. He understood that humans on Earth were so, so small in the vast Universe that stood before them. There was no way they were going to exploit or conquer this frontier, no matter how much they tried, and no matter how much money they possessed. And though beautiful, it was a war zone out there. They couldn't infer what each of these individual galaxies consisted of, or if *Homeland* could survive in them if it could even make it there.

As the ship lulled, he felt it drifting. At this point in time and distance, this is what they needed it to do. They chose not to venture out any further away, until they were able to test the surrounding areas right at the edge of the galaxy.

Arcturus gently squeezed around his mother before letting go, swimming back to the control room. He saw the red light blinking, and was sure that mission control was standing by, panicking from the lack of response. He connected the feed.

It took a moment for the screen to hook up, static for a while before a clear image appeared of mission control, the entire team that worked with them throughout the years standing by. As he stared into the monitor at them, the whole room went up in roars. They were cheering.

"You're alive!" one of them shouted, advancing forward.

Arcturus looked down at himself before he grinned widely, a small laugh escaping his lips as it began to hit him. He inhaled in disbelief as an overwhelming wave pulsated over his body. They had completed the distance of their mission.

Lawlston, who had been their doctor since day one, had admittedly been one of his closest mentors from Earth. He stepped forward from the crowd.

Arcturus placed both hands on the counter before him, peering into the screen at Lawlston. He studied his face a moment, realizing that broken blood vessels polluted the whites of his eyes. At first he thought that it could be from lack of sleep, though a closer look confirmed he'd been crying.

"Viona? Where's my dear Viona?" Lawlston

asked, clearly just beginning to catch his breath as well.

"She's—" Arcturus' voice cracked. "She's been in the corridor, staring. Staring at the Universe? I can't get her to speak. She's happy, she's so happy." His words jumbled over each other.

"Have you been able to measure anything?"

"No—I haven't gotten a chance. We've only just got—do you want to see it? Do you want me to put my suit on?" His words spilled involuntarily out of his lips.

"Arcturus. You need to calm down."

"Calm down?" he shouted, leaning into the screen.

Lawlston put his hand up to his mouth, his eyes wide.

"Arc—"

"We have so much to do, we have to recalculate our supply of fuel because there's no harnessing asteroids out here. How's our ship holding up? Feels about the same in here... of course I've shut off the generators. We're currently drifting until—"

"ARCTURUS!" Lawlston shouted at him, immediately silencing him.

He sat, wide eyed, staring at the screen.

Lawlston had his attention now. "I can't see your mother's pulse."

"What?" he spat, he didn't understand.

Lawlston held up the tablet in his hand. "She's gone, Arc," he said, turning his head. His lip quivered.

"What do you mean, she's gone?" His voice was low. He should have proved them wrong right away, but he didn't want to believe it was true to begin with. "We're not hooked up to monitors, you never had me hook up my vitals to the system." He patted down his chest and lifted the sleeve of his arm, as if to prove to them that he was never hooked up to monitors.

Arcturus looked over his shoulder at the corridor he was just hugging his mother in. He wanted to go to her, to show them that she was right there, looking out the windows at the wonders of their lives.

I don't understand! I don't know what the hell they're talking about.

"Not you. When Viona broke her shoulder, I had her hook up and track her vitals so I could monitor," he said, a little more calmly. "And you need to go to her now," he finished.

Arcturus let go of the swivel chair he was clutching and floated back from the screen. He stared for one moment longer, then he turned and paddled himself to the hallway.

"Mom?" His voice cracked, and he peered around the corner into the doorway. There lay his tiny, frail mother, the human being who taught him everything he needed to know about life itself, and growing, and love.

"Mom!" he shouted at the top of his lungs, burning his throat. "Noo! Mom, NO!" The emotion building up in his gut had forced its way up as a lump in his throat, his eyes immediately blurring. He kicked off the wall and flew towards her, scooping up her body. He pulled her head to his chest and held her, rocking her back and forth as they hovered in the corridor.

Viona looked up at him and blinked her eyes, wincing in pain.

"I… I can't…" she whispered, her voice shaking.

"It's okay, Mom. Shhh... It's going to be okay."

He could see the lump of a tear in the corner of her eye fill up before it escaped away as its own being. "Look how far we've come, Mom?" he asked her, his voice wispy and at the top of his range. "And you were here to see it! You did this. You got us here." He saw a small tug of a smile.

"I... don't want to leave you," she whispered, and he felt a pang of guilt in his chest.

I don't want her to feel that way about me. I don't want her to be in pain.

He thought about the fact that Lawlston said she was gone already, yet here he was, in the corridor, holding his mother as she spoke to him. He looked around the hall and noticed the bracelet mission control used to track her pulse had trapped itself in a corner with nowhere else to go. She ripped it off her wrist when he was in the control room. He imagined she did it on purpose, because she wanted her last moments alive to be just for him, where he didn't have to share them with anyone else. He could keep this time all to his own, because mission control thought he had already lost her. He looked down at her in his arms.

"Mom, it's okay."

She moaned.

He held her. "I am... I am giving you permission to let go. I'm going to be okay."

She moved her head to nod before her body began to convulse in his arms. He held her tightly, turning his head away as he scrunched up his face. He held her until he felt the tension release from her body.

And he knew that it was only him in that graphene lined corridor, the Universe surrounding him as he held the shell of his mother.

He dropped his arms, letting her go away from him, and watched as she began free floating in space, her eyes wide and frozen in time.

No matter what he did, he knew she was gone, as the Universe looked down upon them. She had stayed long enough to see what she had given her life to see, and then she was gone.

"I'm alone now."

The realization sunk into his bones, heavy and unnerving.

He looked away from her limp body, floating in zero g. He inched towards the control room with fluid motion, where he knew everyone would be waiting. His eyes bloodshot and the color drained from his cheeks, he mentally placed a shield between himself and the Universe. His eyes turned to stone, and the emotion dissipated from his expressions.

He caught sight of the eyes on the screen, each one of them staring into him.

"Arcturus... " As Lawlston spoke, Arcturus

moved himself up to the panel, clinging onto eye contact.

"You're going to be all ri-what, what are you doing? NO! Stop, no don't discon—"

Arcturus brought his hand down on the motherboard, and the screen went black.

I'm done. I'm not going to listen to what anyone has to say, because...

"... None of you know how this feels."

Nobody in that room had to hold their mother's dead body, or somehow think of what to do with her. Nobody in that mission control room has to spend the rest of their lives in a ship by themselves, with no human interaction for thirty or more years.

He scanned around the control room for the case that floated away from him earlier that evening. He found it pushed into the far corner, and reached towards it. The thick, puffy flight suit unraveled itself out of the case, the suit that would protect his body when he opened the doors of the ship.

There was nothing quick about suiting up. He unzipped and stripped out of the flight suit he was wearing. He wasn't going out there long enough to wear a diaper like he needed to when they did extensive space walks, but he pulled on the long john pants and long sleeved shirt, along with the layer that held the body temperature control system.

His body curled down to his toes as he adjusted the long john pants, tight at his ankles. When he lifted to look for the legs portion of the suit, he caught a glimpse of himself in a mirror that hung in the frame of the control room. He paused.

Dark curly locks on his head that were getting almost too long. Pale complexion. A strong upper back and shoulders but lacking confidence. He looked just like his father. Viona's words resonated in his mind:

"He didn't want to continue anymore. I could see the pain behind his eyes. He didn't want to wait around to see me pass, and for him to leave you."

He couldn't recall a single time growing up when he saw his parents argue, though he didn't see much conversing either. Dex was a quiet man. He was a man of few words. This made the decision to end his life much harder for Arcturus to understand.

He stretched forward and pulled the bottom half of the Extravehicular Mobility Unit, the EMU, toward him. He looked down into the legs and pictured Dex putting himself into the suit for the last time. Each leg, one at a time. He scooted his bottom half into the legs, then attached the torso section of the suit, buttoning them together. Viona spoke in his mind once more,

"So he went to work on the exterior wall, untethered himself, and let go. He just... let go."

He reached for the helmet and snatched it out of the air, fastening it over his head and pulling down on the visor to bring it into place. He preferred having a smaller helmet, one that made it easier to move around in, and see all angles around his body.

At what point did he know he wasn't coming back? Why even suit up?

He double-checked all the fastenings on the suit, also checking his waist belt for the tethers.

He was ready. Though he wasn't sure exactly, if he was ready to do what he had to do.

He wiggled his fingers inside the gloves to feel the limitations of his mobility in the suit. Everything in the room appeared to be secure and fastened. As his eyes scanned over the control panel of the ship, he saw the blinking red light. It blinked in two different places. He stared at it in a daze, his eyes blurring as he thought about the task that lay ahead. Mission control was desperately trying to get ahold of *Homeland*. He turned from the panel and headed towards the corridor.

When he reached Viona, he scooped her up, and held her like a baby in his arms. Her head hung limply over his arm, and he could not bear to look down at her as he carried her to the door of the ship.

She was the last human he would have contact with for a long while.

I love you so much. And I know you would want it this way.

Arcturus approached the door to the airlock and yanked on the lever with his free hand. He looked down at the clip attached to his waist to double check that the tether rope was connecting him to *Homeland*.

Viona wouldn't need one.

When he secured the lever downward, he used the muscles in his shoulder to twist the wheel. Then to the next door. With a mechanical groan, the door backed out before opening up to the darkness. Holding onto his mother with one arm, he used the other to swing around and rope the tether to a metal rod fastened to the top of the door.

The tether crossed the palm of his gloved hand as he let it out, moving himself and Viona further away from *Homeland*.

His breath was prominent inside his helmet. He listened to his own tensioned breaths.

He only had about thirty seconds with her before nature took its volatile course on her unprotected body, so he acted quickly and built up the courage to look down at her face.

She could have died long before this day. But she held out until she accomplished her life goal, almost as if she had a choice in death.

"I love you, Mom." Arcturus sniffled, his eyes becoming blurry as tears surfaced. He gave himself momentum away from the ship, but remained connected to *Homeland* by the tether that allowed him out a quarter of a mile. He dropped his arms down and gave her body a gentle push away from their galaxy into the Universe.

"I will always have you with me," he told her as the momentum of his push carried her further and further away. He wanted desperately to wipe away his tears, but the bulk of the protective helmet kept him from doing so. Instead he shut his eyes tightly, and opened them again, sizable droplets making their way out of the ducts of his eyes.

He watched Viona's body disappear into the distance before turning to head back to the ship. He was quite a ways out, and he took his time making his way back. He swam, gently flipping his body into a 360-degree turn, hanging onto the tether as the weight of the future rotated inside his mind.

As he watched the Universe, mostly *Homeland*, rotate around and round in his line of sight, he felt the tether vibrate in the palm of his hands. At first what seemed to be just in his mind suddenly became clear; the tether was moving in his gloves. Without further hesitation, he choked up on the rope and pulled, getting himself to the door of the ship as quickly as the tether would allow.

His mind got little time to rest before his instincts kicked in. He was hanging by a thread outside the protection of *Homeland*. If something had gone wrong, he needed to get back. Now.

A pang of adrenaline rushed through his ribcage, and the repercussions of shutting out mission control began to surface. They would have noticed something wrong before he did more than likely.

He pulled on the rope desperately, moving slowly towards the ship. As he reached for the lever, the ship jolted in place, as if it'd revved to life on its own.

It was in that moment, he knew what happened. He had input the codes to have *Homeland* move again on a timer. This was bad.

The motion backfired into the tether, and Arcturus lost his balance. The tether slipped from his grip, and twisted his body like a rag doll.

Even though he was securely clipped to the tether, he didn't want to lose his grip. The last thing he wanted was to involuntarily get dragged by the beastly ship.

In the midst of lack of body control, instead of reaching for the skinny tether, he was close enough to grab onto the lever of the door in mid-spin. The protective helmet smacked against the frame of the door. His neck snapped forward. The front of his forehead came in brief contact with the inside of his helmet, and instantly formed a hairline crack along the high impact-resistant plastic, spider webbing across the material in front of his eyes.

He desperately held onto the doorframe and kicked himself in. Hot, sticky, liquid oozed from his brow and over his closed eyelid. With one eye open, he swung himself into the ship and began slamming the keypad on the control panel to shut the door. As the door slid into place, all he could see was red.

CHAPTER EIGHT

Stitches

His vision went from red to black to red again. With only one useful eye, *Homeland* became a blur as he felt his way through the graphene-lined tunnel to the artificial gravity compressor. He waited for what felt like a century as the floor appeared beneath his feet. His knees weakened and he held onto the wall as he pushed his way into the sleep room.

His temperature rose as he reached up and twisted his cracked helmet off, tossing it to the floor. Putting his hand up to his head, he applied pressure to the bone above his eye with his glove, sighing deeply, his stomach woozy as he fell back with a sense of relief.

"Ahh—" He breathed through gritted teeth. His head swayed, and he fell backwards, almost as if in slow motion. He released the pressure on his brow, dizzy, as his eyes threatened to roll into the back of his head.

Darkness clouded his peripheral vision.

"Come... on!" he growled, frustrated with his vision and balance. He needed to stay conscious. There was no one out there to help him but himself.

He looked at his gloved hand, the deep crimson blood stains seeping into the fabric, a bold contrast against the white.

He shook off the gloves, one at a time. He curled his fingers into a fist, squeezed, and then stretched them back out again. Then he crawled on his hands and knees over to the steel drawers in the wall.

He pulled the bottom drawer open and grabbed a rectangular medical kit. Cracking open the box, he retrieved the hand towel on top and brought it to his brow. The towel sopped up all the blood that poured from the wound.

He sat up, his head heavy, and looked into the medical kit. On top was a mirror, which he took out and magnetized to the steel drawers in front of him.

He removed the towel from his head, some of the fibers catching in the wound and pulling the tattered skin. Wincing, he looked up at the mirror.

It was bad.

Deep.

He closed his eyes and released the breath he had been holding. He pulled out a small pouch of alcohol from the kit and broke the seal. Using the only white part of the fabric left, he squeezed the liquid on, then used it to clean up his face around the wound.

Arcturus yelled out into the ship in pain.

His cry bounced off the corners of the room and echoed back to him. It was much quieter in *Homeland* when the ship was dormant and the engine wasn't working to transport.

He looked down into the kit and pulled out a set of tools that were individually wrapped for sanitation. He crinkled off the wrapper of a needle and thin black thread.

"Serious... no New Skin glue?"

Stitching was old fashioned.

He leaned back for a moment before he lifted his head to look in the mirror. The gash was clean enough to see the split. The shining tip of the needle neared his brow. As he held it closer and closer, the needle trembled in his grasp.

"Steady... "

He struggled with his mirror image. Every movement of the needle betrayed his commands. He gritted his teeth as the pressure built in his mind, finding that the needle was going away from the point he needed it to go.

He looked away from the mirror, relaxed his shoulders, and stretched his neck to both sides.

When he brought his attention back to the mirror, this time he deceived his reflection by offering reverse movements. His empty hand reached up and pinched the skin of the wound together. He brought the needle up to his brow and touched the cold, sterile, device to his skin.

I can do this. I have to do this.

He hesitated, the needle quivering. Then he pierced it through. From one flap of skin to the other, he pulled the thread through.

Despite the pain that blinded him, he sutured the wound to the end of the gash, abandoning the mirror and using his other hand for reference. When he was finished, he laid the thin, bloodied needle back into the kit, and allowed his muscles to finally relax.

With his head flat on the ground, he stared up at the mural on the ceiling of his sleep room. His mother hand painted the strokes of orange and yellow for the depiction of Earth's sky that he'd looked up at his entire life.

I'm alone now.

In his mind his parents argued over the gray shading she chose for the clouds. *They're more white with a golden hue,* his father argued. Viona shot back with, *these are the clouds you see right after there's been a rain shower.* As if weather was so important to the two of them. As if the way he perceived clouds in the sky depended completely on this mural alone. The clouds didn't matter. What mattered was the emphasis on educating him about everything they knew.

This woman was the reason for my existence. She taught me everything. She is the sole reason for who I am today. And now she's gone? She can't be gone.

He traced the lines of the clouds with his eyes. Each brush stroke was neat and intentional, until he came upon a single curve that faltered. The curve aggressively stuck out as a straight line. He wouldn't have noticed it if he didn't know it was there. As Viona came upon that billow in the sky, Dex came up behind her and tickled her down from the ladder. He remembered her kicking her legs as his father held securely onto her waist. He remembered her giggling, and how at six years old, he couldn't help but laugh himself.

The sleep room was much quieter today.

I know that I have a long journey ahead of me. A long, lonely, desolate, journey. My biggest fear is being left alone with my thoughts. Being left alone.

His arms and legs felt full of sand, and his eyelids drooped over half his sight. He couldn't move. He watched his rib cage rise and fall in front of him.

This was it. What he was experiencing would be his life. A tightening caught his throat as his sight began to blur, welling up with tears. Then he cried out. As loud as his body could take, he wailed into the silence of the ship until he needed to take another breath. Tears chased one another down his cheeks, and he sniffled, his breath shaky. No more holding it in. It was time to let go.

He cried until his temples ached, and he began to heave dryness. His tears were gone. As he lay in the middle of the ship, curled into a ball, he heard a faint alarm slowly fading from his parents sleep room, the next room over. It made a *bloop* noise, repeatedly, as it got louder and louder.

He rolled over onto his stomach and pushed himself up onto all fours. Using what strength he could muster, he crawled towards the door. He reached up and scanned his hand on the pad, sliding the door open. The constant noise became louder. He used the doorframe to pull his weak body up to standing. He stopped and listened closely, trying to locate the source of the noise. He heard it coming from their bed area, and he made his way over, stopping before it. The beeping noise was coming from inside the bed.

Arcturus leaned over and lifted the mattress. In the center of the box spring, there was a small, rectangular, black box, with one single green light blinking. He leaned in and picked up the box with both hands. He recognized the small black box as a hologram interpreter. His parents used them throughout his childhood for different lessons, so he could use the hologram to grasp sizing of objects they couldn't show him in reality. There was a message inside.

Why have I never seen or heard this box before now?

He moved to the center of the room and set it on the floor.

Must have been on a timer.

He hesitated a moment before he pressed the green button, holding it down until a bright light projected from the side.

He looked through his swollen, puffy eyes at the holograms of his parents. Younger. His mother was beautiful. She had dark brown, almost black hair that curved at her chin, a milky white complexion with dark facial features, and she was hugely pregnant. In the image she had a big, healthy, round belly that both hands rested on. His father, whom he hadn't seen in years, was standing next to her.

Dex had his arm wrapped around the small of her back. His hair was shaved close to his head, with a closely cut beard covering the bottom half of his face, and his black-rimmed glasses. His body was very fit, with more muscles than Arcturus.

Viona waved at him and smiled, looking at Dex and then back to her son.

Dex exhaled sharply and took a step backwards. He looked down at his mom's belly.

"What do we say?" she spoke, giggling as she looked to Dex for comfort and a suggestion, and Arcturus jumped in the sleep capsule, startled by the sound of her voice.

"Well, just say whatever you want to say. Say

what you feel. You're better at that than I am," Dex replied, leaning in and kissing her head. He placed his hand over hers on her stomach. Viona looked back ahead.

She looked right into him. "Happy 30th Birthday, my dearest child," she said, smiling.

"How can you t—" Arcturus started to say, when he was cut off.

"We are so proud of how far you have come," Dex said, his smile faded as he looked at him as well.

Arcturus was reminded again that they were just a holograph. This was a recording. They weren't real. He couldn't have a real conversation with them, he would just have to listen.

"We know this must be hard for you, Arc. But you were meant to do this." Viona spoke quietly. "As you grow inside me, I can feel that you are special. You are going to be the one that can save everyone's future."

His bottom lip began to quiver, listening to his parents speak.

"No!" He yelled at the holograph, surprising even himself. The outburst echoed back to him. He bit his lip. "*You* don't have to be alone. *You* don't have to sit on the other side of the screen and watch *mankind* live their lives. Fall in love. Have a family. Make a career choice. I don't get that!! I will never have that!! You *stole* it from me!" he yelled at his parent's projections. His throat stung. It was dry.

The fragments of light that made up their bodies began to lightly blink.

Dex began, "You have the ability to change the future of mankind, Arcturus. But only *you* can make that decision. You will find that even though you were born into a highly isolated situation, and under very rare circumstances, it all comes down to the choices you make."

"And we can only hope that you make the right decision. Between what is best for you, and what is best for Earth," Viona finished. Dex added,

"And we hope that you can find peace. We hope that you will forgive us, for giving you this life."

Arcturus sat on the floor, watching them and listening. He had a lot to think about, and a lot of time to think about it.

The images began to blink once again, as the recording came to an end.

"We're almost out of time on the recording," Viona whispered over to Dex. He squinted his eyes at the box, as if trying to read the small numbers on it.

"Right. Well, say your goodbyes then," he told her.

"Arc, we just wanted to wish you a happy birthday. And I want you to know that I have loved you from the moment I discovered you were growing inside me, and I will love you for eternity. Whenever you feel alone or lost, look ahead and you will find us." She lifted the palm of her hand up to her lips, kissed her hand, and blew the kiss towards him.

"Happy Birthday, Son. I love ya," Dex added, and the lighted images were sucked back down into the box, and it was over.

He picked up the box and hugged it to his chest.

"Look ahead and you will find us," he whispered, the weight of the words heavy on his heart.

CHAPTER NINE

Reconnected

Arcturus abandoned the box on the floor of his parents sleep room and went into his own, crawling up onto his bed. He turned onto his side and peered out the window to the exterior. He watched as *Homeland* drifted. The ruffled grayed clouds of a close by dwarf galaxy lay as a satellite of the Milky Way in the distance, the closest bit of light to him.

There is life other than we know it in those other galaxies. It's inevitable. There's no question.

He exhaled deeply from his lungs, deflating his chest.

"But everyone I've ever loved is gone." He spoke aloud to himself, deciding that the echo of his own voice was more satisfying than the silence he was enduring.

His parent's view of death was calculated.

Because you have nothing to look forward to in death, you have everything to live for...

She'd told him a dozen times.

"People are so selfish. Earth has never been my home, yet I am one of them. Am I? I come from the same biological makeup, but am I really one of them?" He sat in silence for a moment.

"Look ahead and you will find us," he repeated yet again, the words from his parents' hologram.

"They have no control over what I do. Absolutely no control. What is keeping me from looking ahead? What is keeping me from steering *Homeland* forward, and never looking back? The possibilities of finding another galaxy where life can sustain are inevitable! Earth is one small, tiny planet. Even the red dwarf I was named for is much larger. And much more solitary... yet it survives. What is keeping me from disappearing from Earth's radar?"

And then it hit him. He scrambled in his bed and got himself up to standing. He looked straight ahead in the capsule, his insides tingling, feeling an energy he needed to release. He spoke the name aloud, into the capsule, his spirits rising as if the word alone was sweet music to his ears.

"Diamandis."

Her golden hair swayed in front of his line of sight as he made his way through the ship. He pushed off a wall and flew into the control room, sliding the door shut behind him. When he began to drift away from the control panel, he grabbed onto the back of the chair and shoved the lever to bring up the QED.

The screen began to fuzz, indicating it was reading his message to connect. But it wasn't connecting.

"Come on!" he growled through gritted teeth. He smashed his hand down on several other buttons. The screen turned white. Mission control began to come into view.

Every person he'd ever worked with stood in the frame. Lawlston looked as though he hadn't slept in days, with deep sunken eyes and a colorless complexion.

Commands were shouted every which way, trying to stabilize the feed as the image became clearer.

As this was going on, the only thing he could focus his attention on was the small, blond-haired, blue eyed, woman staring up at him with a smile on her lips.

The rest of the room was a blur. He placed his index and middle fingers on his lips as if he were 'shushing' them.

Diamandis was aware he wasn't shushing them, and her eyes welled up as she brought her own two fingers up to her lips.

He laughed out loud, exhilarated that she remembered. That it was real.

"Arcturus! Arc, can you hear us?" Leo shouted out to him. When there was no response, he turned to one of the engineers,

"Try and see if you can get voice feed connected? He can't hear our voices."

Arcturus grabbed at his headset and pulled the microphone to his lips.

"I can hear you." His voice was monotone as they all hushed.

"Are you... how is everything?" Lawlston stepped forward and asked, not sure what the response would be.

"Everything's great." The sarcasm was killing.

"Arc... " he pleaded.

This conversation could go two ways. I can con-

tinue being a smart ass and explain to all the world watching that I just finished holding my dead mother before releasing her into the Universe, then came back in the ship, sutured up my own head, then sat and wallowed in my own thoughts about the fact that I will forever be alone from here on out until I'm an old man.

But that's not what they want to hear.

"Everything is under control. I just got back from my mother's funeral."

"Our condolences, Arcturus. We are very sad about your mother's passing. I loved her like a sister." The pain in Lawlston's eyes was genuine.

"What in the world happened to your eye?" He moved closer to Arcturus on the screen.

"S'nothing. I hit it when coming back in *Homeland*. Made a crack in the helmet."

Diamandis' hand reached up and covered her mouth in surprise.

"Get closer, let me take a look at those sutures." Lawlston demanded, motioning him closer.

"Naw, it's fine. In front of everyone? I used the kit in my sleep room... " He rolled his eyes, defeated, and moved closer to the screen. He closed the eye with the gash and afterwards leaned back.

"Well done! Just remember to keep it clean," he said, when Arcturus backed up, nodding his head yes.

"I know, I know. I need to speak with your intern," he said, looking at Lawlston, half smiling at the fact that she was standing right behind him.

"Dia's right here." Lawlston backed up, motioning to her.

"I'd like some privacy."

"Oh... " Lawlston narrowed his eyes. "Well, all right?"

Diamandis stepped forward.

"I'll just... " She pointed to the door, as if she was indicating she'd pick him up on a different feed. Leo stepped in front of her.

"No—we just gained connection back with *Homeland* after all this time of wondering if he'd ever come back! We need to do a data transfer and—"

"Let him go, Leo. The boy just lost his mother, for God's sake."

"Lawlston... " he breathed, pleading.

"Whatever we need to transfer... it can wait." Lawlston sternly finished.

Arcturus nodded to him. "Thank you," he mouthed.

He watched her move through the people and to

the door. Her body slinking, and his chest tightened, his neck getting hot.

"Turn your feed to four, Arc. Okay?

He nodded, and switched the feed from the control room.

Arcturus waited in the silence. He floated back from the monitor a moment and watched the control panel to see which zone she would be coming in on. He stared at the lights and blinked hard, shaking his head to rid himself of the dryness, and looked back at the lights. Still nothing.

He anchored his hands on the back of the swivel chair and worked his way around it to take a seat. Once seated, he grabbed the belt and buckled it, so he wouldn't be able to float away. This was the longest waiting time of his life.

Then it blinked. Zone 4, just like she told him. He leaned forward and touched the button, then backed up to see the monitor. It took a moment to load the screen, and then she came into view.

"Arcturus?" she called out.

"Yes! Yes I'm here... Dia," he said, and for the first time since Viona died, he began to feel an overwhelming sense flood his body. Vulnerability. He reached his hands up to his chest, unaware of how to handle it. His breathing quickened, and his hands became sweaty.

"I'm so sorry for your loss, Arc. I'm so sorry." Diamandis spoke quickly, reaching her hand out as if she could touch his face.

He nodded. "You don't need to feel sorry for me, Dia. It's gonna be all right." He said, his voice softer and higher pitched than usual.

"I just feel for you," she said sympathetically.

"I know... I know." He smiled up at her through the screen.

"I know that Viona was ready, Arc. She had a full life and accomplished everything she meant to. It's not her I feel for... It's the one she left in her wake." She studied his face.

He shook his head back and forth, feeling pressure behind his eyes.

Stay strong for her. Hold your composure.

"I'll be okay," he whispered. "As long as I have you."

She brushed her hair back behind her ear. She pushed the palm of her hand up to cover her mouth, and when he finished his sentence, she moved her hand over to her cheek. She held her cheek, her hand shaking, as her face reddened.

"I'm not going anywhere." Her eyes were welling. He could see a pool of tears threaten at the base of her cool, blue eyes.

He smiled.

They studied each other's faces. Arcturus traced over every line in her face, from her brow down to her high cheekbones. As he looked at her, she moved her hand up to her eyebrow.

"What happened to your eye? Does it hurt?" she asked softly.

"Er, not so much anymore. It did when I had to stitch it up. I wish they'd had some of the New Skin glue in there, instead of a needle and thread," he answered.

"Ouch," she replied, "You said you knocked your head into your helmet?"

"Yeah, it's damaged now. It was close, because it cracked my helmet, but no air was able to escape through the cracks. For a moment I thought I was going to join my mom," he answered.

"Damn. I'm glad you're okay!"

He laughed.

"What's so funny?"

"You're cute. When you're worried, you know."

She huffed, crossing her arms over her chest.

"Well I don't want to be worried." She pouted, scrunching her nose. Arcturus laughed again.

"Please just stay here forever with me?" he asked.

Back to reality...

"Now, you know I can't," she said quietly. He inhaled sharply.

"Sooner or later I'm going to have to go to the bathroom, and eat, and sleep... " She played some more.

"Naw, none of that stuff is important." They laughed together a moment.

"Hey, Arcturus?" she asked.

"Hm?" He heard a noise in the corner of the control room and turned to see a grapple from one of his tethers hitting against the corner of the room, nowhere else to go as it floated. It was insignificant. He brought his attention back to Diamandis.

"Will you just finish doing all the tests mission control has asked you to do?" Her smile had faded, and she was serious. "The whole administration is worried that you've terminated the autopilot when you shut us off last time."

Since Arcturus was born against the will of the *Homeland* Mission's administration, a pregnancy unplanned by anyone but Viona and Dex, UniX programmed the ship on a remote access autopilot to take affect when Viona and Dex both died. They weren't planning on somebody like Arcturus in the ship, able to control the computer over the remote access.

"Why? You on their side now?" he asked, mostly teasing, but curious to find out the answer.

"Arc. You're on their side too. There are no sides. I just feel like they feel you're tossing them around, you know? And so much is at stake with this mission."

"This mission... meaning my life?"

There was a stiff silence between them.

"My whole life I've reported back to that space station. My entire body, inside and out has been charted for everyone to see since I was born. I can't even take a shit without all of planet Earth knowing about it!" Anger caused his hands to shake. His gut was burning, as if he'd start to boil over.

Why is she pressing this matter so deeply?

"Hey! Hey," she yelled, cutting him off. She had his full attention.

He stopped, his heart racing in his chest, pounding to the point that he heard each beat echo off the walls of the control room.

"I only want you to complete your tasks for them so that you can turn that ship around and come back to me," she said quietly, her eyes locked on his. She mesmerized him.

He sighed, looking into her pale, sparkling, blue eyes.

"Lets plan a time to meet later tonight," she said quickly.

"Tonight?"

"Yeah... I'll let you get to work. And then maybe later tonight we can get to work. Together."

His stomach flipped. "I'd like that," he whispered.

"That way... while you're working... you'll have something—" Sitting in her chair, she reached down and moved her shirt up just a little, revealing small portion of her stomach and navel. His eyes trailed down to her stomach.

He gulped.

"—to look forward to," she finished with a sultry smile.

He barely heard her last sentence. "I'll get right to work, Captain." He mock saluted her.

She laughed, dropping her shirt back down, "It's a date then."

His chest warmed as his watched her cheekbones and the freckles that lay across them turn a light shade of pink.

"It's a date."

CHAPTER TEN

Late Night

Arcturus moved into the corridor, his eyes flittering in all directions as he looked through the windows. He stopped a moment and grabbed onto the ledge of the large window with one hand, his tablet held to his chest. He looked out. Another galaxy glowed in the near distance, most likely a small dwarf galaxy. He watched as its dark frothing clouds billowed up around the large, golden sphere in the middle.

He closed his eyes tight and opened them again, his blurred vision focusing on the galaxy once more. No matter how many times he looked away and looked back, the view felt new, as if he could never get used to the sight.

I'm the only human that's ever witnessed this.

The weight of his thoughts bore down on his

chest and wrapped itself around his body, though it wasn't restricting. The tightness in his chest felt exhilarating.

He was the only human to have made it this far in the Universe, and to have lived. A sense of importance washed over him, but was quickly extinguished by the bitterness he often felt when he thought of the mission. Though he loved his parents, he couldn't help but think of the fact that he didn't choose this life for himself.

And if it wasn't for this, he could be down on Earth with Diamandis.

Though if this mission never existed, would I have even met Dia? Would she be interested in me even if I weren't the famous boy born in space?

He turned from the window. The Milky Way was behind the ship, out of his sight. He looked into the corridor realizing in that moment, that the last time he was here, he was holding his mother.

There's nothing more I can do. She's gone.

He moved forward, toward the door to the AGC. A chill that he wasn't expecting slinked up his spine, and it shook him once again. He made it a point to change the gears in his mind to think about where he was headed, rather than wallowing in the past.

Dia. She was going to be waiting for him soon, and he had no idea what to expect, considering their last meeting. The beating in his heart began to pound again, this time as if it was hitting against the inside of his chest cavity. He also consciously felt perspiration form under his arms.

Arcturus waited for the anti-gravity hardware to kick in, his feet joined with the floor underneath, and he moved the palm of his hand over the sensor. The door to the sleep room slid open. He walked through the door, quickly unzipping the flight suit and slipping his arms out of the sleeves. He pushed the suit down to his ankles and walked out of it. Wearing heather gray boxer briefs, he turned to his chest of drawers lined on the wall. He pulled out the top drawer and pushed it up, turning the hinges inside out. A mirror appeared on the other side, and he quickly searched the mirror, staring back at his own reflection.

He rubbed his eyes, staring into the image. He reached his hand up and patted his black, curly hair down, trying to make it lay flat. It seemed a struggle, and he cursed into the air as he gave up his attempt. His curls stood straight up, making his soft hair look frizzed, even when he wasn't in zero g. He stared in at his dark chocolate brown eyes.

What am I doing. Am I trying to look good for Dia?

Yes.

He stared at the stitch job he did above his eyelid.

Not bad.

One of the stitches was crooked but that was because he struggled with getting the needle to go where he needed it to, because the mirror projected a backwards image to him.

He backed up and viewed his body. His bare chest was firm, with only a small patch of dark black hair in the center, as well as a trail from his navel, disappearing under his briefs. His skin was pale, having never seen the UV rays of the sun.

The medical engineers of their mission came up with a replacement for the Vitamin D they would lose from lack of sun exposure, by providing it in the meals they would eat.

Though he imagined that nothing could replace the feeling of the sun on the skin, something that Arcturus was also robbed of.

He blinked into the mirror, shaking his head to rid it of the thoughts that were distracting him. He bent over and pulled open the second drawer from the bottom. In it lay a classic, white flight suit with navy blue patches on the side of the arm—one of the United States flag and one of the UniXplor emblem, something that was sewn onto all of his clothing, and something which he never really paid attention to. He pulled out the suit and quickly shot one leg into it, then the other. He pulled the suit up over his arms and shoulders, zipping up the front. He looked in the mirror again, trying to flatten down the hairs on his head one last time before giving up, and shutting the mirror up into the wall.

The moment he shut the mirror, making a banging noise, the tablet began to blink. He placed a hand on his stomach as it began to churn. His breathing quickened.

He ran over to his bed and placed the tablet flat on the end of it, clicking it into place. He backed up onto the bed and sat with his legs crossed, up against his pillow. Very quickly, the tablet projected a screen that lit up the whole room, which was otherwise dark except a few glowing lights on the walls to allow navigation.

Arcturus took a long, deep breath into his lungs, expanding his chest, as the light pixilated itself into the image of the space station.

"Hi."

He smiled, lifted his hand and waved back to her.

Her hair was down, one side draped over her shoulder. It was straight, and more golden than ever. She wore a button-up black shirt and blue jeans, with a slim, white doctor's coat over that.

He curiously examined her body, her curves. He'd occasionally seen people in mission control wearing clothing like this, and he'd never paid much attention to it before. In *Homeland*, he'd always worn the same thing. It was always a space suit, one of the large ones that he wore on the exterior of the ship, or one of the thin fabric ones that he wore for daily use in the ship. His mom wore them, his dad wore them, and Arcturus began to wear his father's suits as well, once he was gone.

But Diamandis was wearing Earth clothes. And he was very much interested in them now, with her wearing them. He liked the black button up.

"Are you working?" he asked, a smile still on his lips. He felt warm, and excited to be speaking with her. He'd just spent the entire day alone in the ship, something he'd have to get used to sooner than he wanted, and it was nice to finally get back to seeing her.

Not just anybody... but her.

"Well... Oh," she said, looking down and pulled the doctors coat away from her chest. "Yeah, I just got off," she said, smiling, "I forgot to put my coat back in the closet."

"Do they know you're talking to me?" he asked. She laughed.

"Does it matter?"

"No I guess not." He shrugged.

"I'm kidding... I told Lawlston I was staying late so he logged it that I was doing background research in... " She lifted her hands and spun around in the large, high-backed, swivel chair she sat in. He leaned in to view the room she was sitting in. It looked like a large laboratory. It had long tables to the side, with different models of the cardiovascular system and pulmonary veins.

"Oh yeah... " He stopped for a moment, looking around behind her.

"I think I've seen this room before—long time ago though. It was part of anatomy in my secondary training."

"Would that be like... high school?" she asked and their laughs intertwined, creating a harmonious melody.

"Yeah, I guess you could say that. Different content though. I don't know what high school is like."

"Well you don't know the social part, right?" she asked.

He shrugged, not entirely sure what she meant by *the social part*.

"Yeah, the cafertery is pretty lonely," he joked.

"Cafertery?"

"Yeah, that time when you stop doing school work and everybody eats things that are all different from each other."

"Oh, the cafeteria?" She asked, narrowing her eyes, a smile creeping up on her lips.

"Oh," He said quietly, the back of his neck warming. Diamandis laughed.

He smiled, then laughed along with her.

"Man, your laugh," he said

"What?" she asked, pulling her head back to look at him.

"Nothing, your laugh is just so cute." He laughed again.

"Now I'm going to think about it!" She swatted her hand at him.

"No, please... don't. Just be yourself."

"Arc," she whispered, moving her chair closer

to the monitor.

"Hm?" he asked, watching her every move.

"Am I the first girl you've ever met?" she asked quietly, her lips thinning. She blinked her eyes at him, and he looked right into her irises, realizing that they were the perfect shade of blue; straight from the center of the most beautiful cosmic nebula he'd ever seen. He wondered if the ocean looked that same shade of blue from the ground.

"Am I?" she asked again.

He was brought out of his trance. He shook his head.

"Sorry... Uhm, no? You're not the first girl I've ever met. I've lived for thirty years," he said, flat out and blatantly.

She sat back.

"I'm sorry... I didn't mean for it to sound like that," he said softly. "I've met many girls. You are the first girl I've been drawn to. Dia, you are so attractive." He redeemed himself.

"You are the first girl I've ever been *with*." He clarified.

"Well if I'm the first girl you've ever been with, how do you know that you want to be with me?"

He moved forward on the bed, closer to the

screen, ready to play her dangerous game. He watched her move her hair off her shoulder. "I know what I want."

She remained quiet and moved her arms to cross them over her stomach. She looked up at Arcturus, and he saw the flames in her eyes, roping up and around her pupils. She reached up and unbuttoned the first button on her shirt. She looked back up at him.

He sat and watched, his knees beginning to shake, and hoping they were not visible on the camera. She didn't seem to notice. The corner of his mouth twitched up into a smile. He reached his hand up to the zipper on his flight suit and unzipped it down to his navel, revealing his chest. Diamandis watched him, looking over his body.

She looked up to his face. She unlatched the second button to her black shirt and pulled it open, revealing a plain black bra underneath.

He swallowed hard. An uncomfortable tightening in his pants arose as he traced his eyes along the edge of her bra.

Is this wrong? Could someone be watching us? She wouldn't reveal herself so freely to me if we were being watched.

He looked from her bra up her collarbone to her face. As he stared into her swirling blue eyes, the entirety of *Homeland* around him melted away. He was no longer in the ship.

He was right in front of her.

He put his hand up to her chest and unbuttoned the final two buttons of her shirt, one after the other.

She first looked down at her stomach, and then back up into his eyes.

He met her gaze once more before making another move. "May I?" he asked politely.

"Yes," She whispered, leaning into him with her eyes closed.

He put his hand up on her arm and pushed the shirt off her shoulder, then the other, and let it fall to the floor behind her. He looked down at the curvature of her breasts and breathed deeply.

He reached out and placed his hand on her waist, halfway between her chest and hips. As he looked back to her face, her eyes were looking down.

Her long eyelashes fluttered as she brought her gaze up to his face, her lips slightly parted. She stepped in between his feet, bringing herself closer to him and more comfortably in his grasp. She leaned in, her soft cheek against his, and he smelled the white tea and citrus in her hair. He closed his eyes, allowing them to roll into the back of his head.

Diamandis stepped up on her tiptoes, and whispered in his ear. "Arc... " Her breath was hot on his ear. "Take off your suit." The words flicked off her tongue with ease.

It made him dizzy, made him want her.

Arcturus opened his eyes, and pushed back from Diamandis as everything began to melt around him again, dissolving before his eyes. He blinked several times as the silver sheen of the ceiling in his sleep room came into view. He looked to his left out the small window above his bed, confirming that he was still aboard *Homeland*, where he had been all along.

He looked up at the monitor that projected from the tablet on his bed. Diamandis looked breathtaking in her black bra, the black button-up shirt thrown on the floor behind her. She still wore her blue jeans, though they were unbuttoned and unzipped, the fly fanned out as she sat. She looked down at herself.

"What's wrong?" she asked quietly.

For the first time he thought he sensed a trace of insecurity in her voice.

"Oh, uh, uh nothing." He choked over his words, realizing his neck and shoulders were tense, and he reached down to adjust his crotch. "I don't know about... " He started, and she turned and reached back for her shirt.

"No! It's okay... it's just—" he began as she scooped up the shirt.

"I'm sorry. I shouldn't have come on to you like that. I don't know what I was—"

"You're so beautiful." He spoke quickly, his voice soft. "And I want to be here with you. I just wish I could be right there with you... How are we going to?" he asked, unsure of where they were going to go, and angry with himself for stopping wherever it was that they were going.

They shared a silence between them before she spoke.

"You just... " she began in a whisper; gaining back the confidence she had before, the confidence that he had found so sexy. "... Let it happen," she finished, carefully setting her shirt back down on the floor. She sat in the seat.

He watched her stomach. It was flat as she stood, and her ribs moved up and down quickly with her breathing. He saw that her heart rate was fast. He felt his own heartbeat in his chest, and his breathing shortened as he became more nervous.

He reached up and slipped his arms out of the suit, allowing it to fall behind him.

He watched her as she looked down at his chest. He wondered if she noticed the black hair that trailed from his navel down. She looked back up at his eyes. He saw her cheeks blush, and it made his own face warm.

He leaned back in his bed and slipped the suit down to his ankles, gently maneuvering the fabric off his feet. He sat in his boxer briefs and looked back up at her for her direction as to where to go next. He couldn't stop staring at her chest.

Without saying anything, Diamandis stood up. Her face was off the monitor, with only her stomach and waist in view. She placed her hands on the sides of her jeans and moved her hips back and forth, slinking the jeans down to her ankles. She stepped out of them and backed up so her full body to was in the view of the monitor. She stood there. Her underwear was black like her bra, and also lacy, full lace, and he saw through to her skin.

"You... " he breathed, exhaling all of his energy. "You are *so* attractive." He was unable to blink as he stared at her body, from her face down to her toes.

She giggled, half circling around her chair as

she sat back down, adjusting the camera on her face and chest.

His eyes focused on her, his peripheral vision blurred once more, blackening out in tunnel vision. He moved in closer to her on the screen.

She reached her hand up to her bra strap and pushed it over her shoulder. It fell down the side of her arm. She did the same to the other side.

Arcturus held his breath, his excitement growing into a ball of energy that hovered just above his stomach.

She squeezed her shoulder forward, the cleavage of her breasts expanding in the bra, making her chest bigger. He noticed that she had a freckle on her left breast, and he couldn't take his eyes off her.

"Do you wa—" she began.

"Yes," he answered quickly, mesmerized.

She laughed softly, reaching her hand up behind her back. He listened carefully, silence in the room behind him, as she unhooked her bra behind her back and let go. She slid her arms easily out of the straps, and the black bra fell to the ground.

He followed his eyes along her chest. Her breasts were petite and they curved up at the nipples, which he noticed were hard. His own hardened.

She shyly tilted her head down and he searched for her eyes.

"Dia... " he breathed.

She smiled.

"You w—" he began, putting his hand on the elastic of his boxer briefs. Before he could finish his sentence, she bit her lip and nodded her head up and down in response. He bent down and pushed off his underwear, inching it down his legs, pulling the hair on his legs as he went. He looked up at her as she watched him, her eyes intense and her teeth biting her bottom lip. He put his arms up and shrugged, implying that this was all of him, all he had to give.

"I... " she whispered, moving closer to the screen. "I love you," she finished.

Arcturus sat back, dumbfounded. He looked from her breasts, to her collarbone, to her jawbone, to her eyes.

"Dia, I love you too," he whispered.

What am I saying?

She looked at him, intensity and vulnerability in her eyes. She touched her hand to her stomach and then moved it down into her underwear. He could not take his eyes off her hand and he watched her as she began to stroke herself, back and forth. He felt the energy running in his arms and his legs, intensifying in his thighs. He watched her as she enjoyed herself, her eyes closed at first before she opened them, looking right into him.

"Just close your eyes and imagine we're together," she told him softly.

"Closing my eyes is the last thing I want to do."

She smiled, then leaned back and began the motions once more. She nodded to him.

He reached down and began to touch himself, taking her lead.

She shook her head yes.

As he stroked, his eyes rolled in the back of his head, and he fought himself to keep his eyes fixed on Diamandis, his hands shaking as he watched her pleasure herself to his motions.

She began to moan, which sent him burning over the edge, and he quickly reached for the flight suit with one hand as he continued the motions. He cupped the flight suit around himself, feeling the warm, thick liquid come seeping into the fabric. He leaned up and tried to catch it all, feeling as though it would never stop.

He looked up at her, watching him, and the moment their eyes met, she arched her back and closed her eyes. She continued to stoke herself, crying out as if it were painful, though she was smiling. He watched her breasts as she bent back, enjoying herself, which in part, made him woozy.

When she was finished, she sat up and slipped her hand out of her pants, leaning over, off camera to grab some paper napkins. She used them to wipe her fingers, looking up at him as he sat there, watching her.

He observed the creases under her eyes, realizing how worn out she looked, and it was the first time he noticed that he had sweat pearling up at his hairline. His neck felt hot, and his mind was soaring. He felt exhilaration in his chest, and he looked at Diamandis as she leaned down and grabbed her shirt, slipping it over her head and neck, over her chest without replacing her bra.

She smiled at him, pulling her hair back and tying it up in a high ponytail with a tie she had on her wrist. She sat a moment in her underwear and shirt, watching him.

"So this must be what gravity feels like on Earth," he whispered, smiling at her.

She raised her brow, a playful smile still painted across her lips. "Hm?" She asked, confused.

"When two things are attracted to each other," he finished, whispering close to the screen.

She laughed to herself, looking up at him with her piercing blue eyes. He sighed, leaning back on the bed. This time he covered his waist up with the flight suit, not allowing her to see the hot, sticky, mess that was underneath when he released. He was exhausted and drained but felt the energy running through his veins, the energy that made him feel like he was floating, and he was floating, way, far away from the world itself.

She leaned forward, close to the screen, her lips full, and soft, and mesmerizing. She looked him in the eyes, deep inside him.

"I forgot to tell you something."

He leaned forward, and despite their literal distance apart, felt close to her in a way he'd never felt close to another human being before.

"Hm?" He asked.

"Happy Birthday, Arcturus."

CHAPTER ELEVEN

Advancing Forward

A rcturus woke in his bed, bare skinned and cold. He turned onto his side, stretching his mouth wide into a yawn. The blanket lay scrunched at his feet, and he reached down to pull it up and over his shivering body, all the way to his neck. He lay in bed, thinking about the previous night and trying to recall if it was just a dream or not.

A smile came to his lips.

Even if it were just a dream, it was the greatest dream of my life.

He moved from his night, to the duties he would be conducting on the ship today, and shifted in his bed.

It's so cold. Much colder than usual.

He shivered in the blankets, and then rolled over onto the floor, groaning from the impact. He crawled over to corner of the room and slid open the door to the lavatories to relieve himself, before finally going to check the temperature of the sleep room. The temperature had dramatically dropped since before he went to sleep.

"Why aren't any alarms going off?" he questioned, hurrying to the drawers to grab some clothing. He barely remembered finishing the zipper on his suit before he rushed out of AGC, and soared across the corridor into the great room. He propelled himself so fast that he slammed into the wall next to the door of the control room.

"Dammit!" he yelled, readjusting himself to enter the control room. He went through the doorway and up to the screen, hitting the QED transmitter back to Earth.

"Mission control, come in. Mission control, do you read me? This is Arc, reaching you from *Homeland*." He was calm and collected; going right into the mode he was trained to be in when he got himself in these situations, as they'd happened before.

"Lawlston! Leo! Come. In," he yelled into the headset. He could hear static.

"Pfft. Arc pfft. Tur pff."

"I can hear you, mission control. Do you copy?"

He tried a few more buttons on the touch control panel to attempt to sharpen the voice.

"*Homeland*, this is mission control, copy." The voice came through his headphones loud and clear.

"I can hear you, mission control. Copy. I can hear you." He responded.

"Arc? Are you there?" It was Lawlston's voice coming in through the headphones.

"Yes. I'm here. I can hear you but I'm not getting an image feed. What's going on?" He spoke quickly into the speaker of his headset.

"Not quite sure yet, Arc. Press D-12 to B. See if that'll... "

He did as he was commanded. An image blurred, then it came through on the monitor.

"There!" Lawlston shouted. "Whatever you just did, that worked."

"What's going on?" Arcturus asked again. "I'm going to have to start the generator, Doc. It's freezing in here." He spoke through chattering teeth.

"I can see the discoloration in your lips. Are you drinking enough water? Go grab one now," Lawlston began, concerned.

"No. It's not dehydration. It's a temperature drop. I'm going to start up the generators and get this ship moving again. I've got enough fuel to last me a while longer," he told Lawlston, ignoring any other commands coming his way.

There was a moment of silence.

"Do what you have to do, Arc," Lawlston said quietly, putting down the electronic chart he held in his hands.

Arcturus stared at the monitor a moment, not sure if he actually heard the words correctly. He usually needed to do more persuading to get his way. He moved the swivel chair and pulled himself onto it. After he buckled himself into the seat and strapped his ankles into the bottom, he got ready to get into gear. The best option was to try and start up the generators, using the fuel harnessed from his last asteroid mining expedition, when he collected enough to last him a month or so, Earth time.

"Do I need to get Leo?" Lawlston asked, keeping his eyes fixed on the monitor.

"Uhh, yeah maybe?" Arcturus responded, pulling his headset closer and looking around at all the controls. "I mean, I've started this thing up so many times, but since it's uncharted territory, we might want a few eyes on this?"

"Right," Lawlston agreed.

"Oh and Doc?" he called out as Lawlston began to proceed to the door.

"Yeah?" He looked over his shoulder.

"Hurry," he said quietly.

Without another word, Lawlston raced out of the room.

Arcturus sat a moment and listened to the gears turning underneath him. The humming was loud as the ship awoke from its slumber, drifting in the space outside the galaxy. Because he was getting used to the quiet, the humming of the generator was overly loud, starting up as if he was standing right next to the propellers of an airplane.

"Arc?" Leo yelled as he slid into the room. "You okay?"

"What's that?" he shouted into the speaker, watching the monitor and adjusting the volume. "Sorry, it's just this thing is so loud."

"Let me adjust the mic here." Leo said.

Arcturus responded, "I've only just started up the engine, I'll begin moving in a second. I can already feel a temperature change. Lawlston?"

"Yes. Your body temperature is up five degrees. That's excellent. Do we need to proceed then?" Lawlston looked down at the chart he held and then back to the screen. "It may be dangerous, Leo. We haven't tested the levels yet to see if his body is capable of proceeding."

"I'll be fine. Really. Any ounce of doubt and I'll turn around." Arcturus tried to convince them. The thought of being able to explore, instead of remaining stationary like he had been for so long, was very appealing.

"Yeah you'll turn around if it's not too late. We can't help you if you're passed out!" Lawlston explained, tapping into his electronic tablet. Leo must have had computer contacts in, because he was shuffling things around in the air with one hand, the other hand on his hip.

"All right, go for it Arc." He nodded his head. He must have been looking through his contacts to *Homeland*.

Arcturus did what he was told. His body was pushed back as he felt the pull from the ship beginning to move. He grinned widely. "We're back in!" he told them, swiping the monitor with their image over to the side and activating the protective shield, opening up the cover to see outside the front of the ship. He sat back and stared in wonder at the spectacular sights before him.

"What is it?" Leo asked, both him and Lawlston leaning in together, probably to see if they could see what Arcturus was seeing.

"It's just... it's incredible," he whispered. He unbuckled himself and floated above the chair, grabbing the webcam and turning it to show them what he saw.

They watched in stunned silence.

"We should be broadcasting this," Leo stated.

"No," Arc interrupted. "Just enjoy it. For one second of your life just sit back and enjoy it. I'm going to engage the engine and advance in a moment."

Leo and Lawlston looked first at each other, then back to the shield.

Arcturus moved his attention to the view outside the ship. He observed the purple, red, and blue swirling lights of the galaxies in front of him, definitely a sight to behold. He couldn't even count the number of swirling galaxies that appeared before *Homeland*.

It was fortunate that space technology advancements in spacecraft design allowed *Homeland* very low odds of impact. It was made so that debris could roll up and over the spacecraft, but not ever smash into it. Throughout his lifetime, there were times where Arcturus accompanied his father in making repairs to the exterior of the ship from general, natural wear and tear of the space vehicle from the number of years it was abroad.

Arcturus managed to bring himself back to the situation, realizing he had zoned out for too long, and that Dr. Lawlston was trying to get his attention.

"Arcturus!"

He shook his trance and focused on the monitor. "S-sorry."

"I'm going to need you to suit up so I can monitor your body functions and vitals as you advance further away from the galaxy."

"Aw-come on, I've al—" he began to protest, when he was sternly cut off.

"You will do as I say. No human has ever before been this far away from Earth, and I need to make sure you're safe."

Arcturus was used to the kindness that Dr. Lawlston always treated him with, and this was definitely a different demeanor. He felt as if Lawlston was trying to take over the father role, which was obviously not going to be productive. But the doctor role, that might be more acceptable to him.

"I don't really have time, Doc," he mumbled, annoyed.

"You have all the time in the world. Nobody's pushing you to move that ship this second."

"Fine," Arcturus said. He unzipped his suit and ripped it off his shoulders, allowing it to hang a moment, his chest bare. He moved his way over to the other side of the control room and pulled open a drawer that latched into the wall. Lawlston watched him through the monitor from behind.

"Grab the silver one," he shouted.

Arcturus briefly looked over his shoulder at him before turning back to the drawer he held onto and started sifting through wires and cords. He pulled out a contraption and shut the door, making his way back to the swivel chair in front of the screen.

He unvelcroed the belt and wrapped it around his stomach, attaching it to the front. Then he grabbed the wires and attached suction cups to different parts of his chest. He also took the temperature gauge and attached it to the side of his forehead, just above his temple.

"Okay, am I good?" he asked, looking up at Lawlston, who was trying to pick up a reading on Arcturus's vital signs. He heard a door open in mission control, and Diamandis walked in. She was wearing all black, with a black Peter Pan collar that folded up over her white, medical, lab coat.

"Sorry I'm late, Doctor Lawlston, traffic was horrible on the 79. Get me up to speed? Oh, Hello Arc!" She turned, her face blushing over the freckles under her eyes as the sight of him on the screen caught her off guard.

Arcturus loosened up and calmed at her presence.

She was called in to work, to help Lawlston with recording his vitals. If he had known that before, he would have suited up with absolutely no problem.

"Diamandis." He nodded hello, allowing her name to roll off his lips like a song. "It's a pleasure to have you here," he smiled.

"I'm sure it is," she smirked back, teasing him in front of her colleagues.

"I'm hooking up his vitals now so that we can monitor them before he advances. Here take this; I'll let you check these gauges, while I'll keep an eye on temperature and reflex response. The other men will have radiation and exterior covered," he finished, catching her up on what was going on.

"Right." She took over as she went to work.

Arcturus watched her as they worked together. Thoughts of last night surfaced, and he couldn't get the image of the curves of her body out of his mind.

She was such a temptation, such a distraction for him on this mission.

What would I do without her? I want nothing but to be with her, around her, in her presence at all the waking hours of my life.

He didn't understand this feeling he was experiencing. And he wasn't sure how he'd lived his whole life leading up to this point without having felt like this.

"All right do you see your panel, Arc? They are giving the go ahead. And all eyes and attention are on you," Lawlston announced.

Arcturus nodded. He leaned back and pulled the suit back up and over all the wires, zipping it up to his neck. He arranged himself back in the swivel chair and strapped his waist and ankles in. In addition to the headset and temperature gauge he had on his head, he also leaned forward and unhitched a helmet and visor that went on his head and over his face, to protect from any disturbances inside *Homeland* that might come his way.

"Ready? Ready. I'm starting the advancement," he announced, not paying attention to the second feed coming in from mission control. His body swayed, even against the lack of gravity, at the motion of the ship being engaged into advancement, *Homeland* moving forward. It felt exhilarating to be moving again. He felt that he had complete control over the spacecraft, and the vulnerability of drifting into the unknown had temporarily subsided.

The ship was moving very fast, faster than any speed that could be comprehensible on Earth. This entire mission had been pre-routed on something sort of similar to cruise control, meaning the route was planned ahead of time, and the ship automatically stayed on that route until they reached outside the galaxy. Outside of the Milky Way Galaxy, they were working with uncharted territory, so it was like driving forward without a map on land that had never been cultivated.

"Arc, what do you see? What does it look like?" Voices came in on his headset.

"Oh it's spectacular. There is no way—and you can confirm this. Put it on the record books. There is no way that we are alone in this Universe. There are more clouds than I can count out here, and all of them have sustainable stars like our own dying sun." He spoke quickly, quietly, and didn't even care who he was speaking to, just that fact that somebody was listening.

KRISTIN HELLING

"You may need to—slow—Arctur—" the voice was starting to cut out, but he was so enraptured in his own advance that he couldn't begin to notice that he was starting to lose feed.

"I'm coming up on some sort of disturbance." He looked ahead.

"I'm going to try and test the elements in the lack of atmosphere here," he began, continuing to do what he pleased.

"Arc! We are losing you. I repea—"

He heard mission control shouting at him. He bounced back. "Oh! I'm sorry, let me try and slow this down here. Can you hear me?" he yelled back, beginning to slam buttons on the touchscreen control panel.

"Leo? Can you hear me?" No answer. He still saw their images on the monitor, running back and forth on the screen; checking computers and shouting back at him, though he could not read their lips.

"I can't hear you! I've lost contact completely in my headset. Mission control, come in. Can you hear me? I repeat. Can you hear me? This is *Homeland* to mission control. I am trying to steer back, and there appears to be a malfunction. I am experiencing

191

resistance. *Homeland* to mission control. Do. You. Copy?"

Then visual was cut.

He could no longer see images from them, only a blank screen.

"Aw shit," he whispered to himself, continuing to try and force the button used to steer." If I can't get this back up, I'll just keep going forward! I've completely lost contact with mission control!"

It was then that he felt a moment of panic in the pit of his stomach. It washed over him, like a bad dream finally coming to life. He began to think of all the possibilities.

If I could steer the ship and could only move forward, I most certainly would find out what was outside our galaxy. But I would begin to lose time.

He wasn't sure how to troubleshoot it, or what he would need to do to fix the problem.

I could attempt to shut off the ship, though that would just make me drift again, which may make me worse off than where I am now!

Then her blonde, golden hair came into his mind.

He could see her icy, blue eyes above her high cheekbones that were spritzed with freckles, which he liked to think of as kisses from the sun.

What if I could never get back?

He felt a pang of hurt in his heart.

What if she was gone forever? What if I never got the chance to ever see her again, to ever be with her again?

He couldn't bear it. He had to see her again.

He wanted to go back.

To end this mission.

There were so many years ahead of him, but the simple thought of turning around, going back through the Milky Way Galaxy, spending the next thirty years in solitude before he would have the chance to touch her, to taste her; everything would be worth it.

His whole life would be worth the wait. Then he could also physically bring back all the information his parents ever dreamed of collecting. He could help Earth, and everyone would be happy. This would be the ultimate ending to the *Homeland* mission, and he would be home, at last!

He had to find a solution.

And he had to find one quickly, because an alarm began to sound throughout the control room.

"What now?" he yelled out to himself, realizing it had gotten quiet despite the ringing sound piercing his eardrums. He found it was beginning to become hard to breathe, his airflow was slowly being cut off. He inhaled sharply, releasing a shaky breath. He needed to move quickly.

The decision to leave *Homeland* was made before he knew how he would do it.

He unbuckled himself and moved over to the edge of the room, ripping open several doors that were latched shut. He grabbed a clear box full of food and liquid pouches and hurled it through the air, through the door of the control room and into the great room. He also grabbed the case that held his exterior walking space suit and tossed that out. He maneuvered up to the control panel and unhitched the tablet, hoping he would be able to somehow use it for transmitting a signal.

With the tablet under his arm, Arcturus used the other arm to push off the wall, floating through the doorframe and into the great room. He swam through the air and retrieved both the case with his suit in it and the tub, and allowed them to float over to the door that lead to his asteroid mining capsule. He slid open the door to the capsule, and moved all the supplies inside. Very swiftly, he was able to move the food tub inside and lock it down against a wall, beside another box of tools.

Next, he attached the tablet onto the control panel, making sure it was safely secured. He figured it would be all right to allow the case with his suit in it to float around the room until he could come back. He turned away from the capsule, going back into *Homeland*.

"Just a few more things," he said to himself, as he headed for the sleep rooms. There were just a few more items he could not leave without.

CHAPTER TWELVE

Fire

'm not leaving without it.

He spun around in the air and swam towards the sleep rooms. He needed to move very quickly. His lungs felt like they were closing in, and with every breath he took, the air seemed thinner. He used all his strength to push off the walls and advance himself in the direction of the sleep rooms. The more he closed in on them, the warmer it seemed to get. He was worried that it was his own body temperature rising, rather that the external properties of the air. He wondered if Lawlston was able to get a reading on his vitals and temperature or if they'd lost contact with his body when they lost complete feed on the QED.

He felt himself become uncomfortable in his suit, his insides boiling and his skin felt dampened by sweat. He emerged into the compressor, the door shut behind him. As his feet met the floor, he was hoping that the heat would subside.

It only got worse.

His head began to sway, his body temperature experiencing two extremes, from waking up freezing to blazing hot. His body weakened. But he knew he had to get to the sleep rooms before he went back to the asteroid mining capsule and back into safety.

Arcturus reached out and slid the door back, opening up into his room. It appeared fine, and he ran past his bed to the next door that led to his parents sleep room. He scanned his hand over the pad on the wall, but the door did not respond to his touch. He groaned, an immediate headache weighing down his temples mixed with dizziness as he tried it again. Again, the light stayed red instead of its usual green glow.

He pushed his stubby fingernails into the crease of the door and used all his strength to pry it open. He was able to get it an inch wide, when a wafting cloud of black smoke escaped through the crack. He backed up, coughing deep from within his lungs. He waved his hand in front of his face to thin out the smoke, and peered through the crack into his parents sleep room. He could make out the blazing colors of red and orange flames engulfing the room.

The room had somehow caught fire.

"No!" he yelled out gruffly, throwing himself at the door and trying to pry it open once more. He balled up his fists and slammed them into the door, banging his knuckles so hard that it dented, and the joints on his fingers began to bleed. He was so fired up from adrenaline that he barely felt the impact.

He was able to get the door open just enough to slip in, and stopped a moment.

Wait. Am I really doing this? Is it worth it?

He needed to get to the space underneath his parents bed where he left the hologram they gave him for his 30th birthday.

I want it.

Just that one thing. And he was willing to risk burning himself in a blazing fire, just so he could bring that with him. It was a little piece of his parents, and when he was in the dark of space, he could have the company of them with him, even if it was only a memory. He squeezed his body through the door, sucking in his chest.

Once inside, he slid onto his knees and skidded to a halt right in front of their bed. He ducked down and reached his hand underneath, retrieving the small black box.

I know this is only materialistic. I know this place is full of just stuff, but... but...

He turned around from the bed and watched the flames rising, arching their way across the ceiling to his own room. He dropped to the floor, hugging the hologram box under his arm as he low-crawled, army-style through the doorframe to his own room.

The flames had already spread. As he lay on the floor, he looked directly above him at the ceiling.

The mural that stretched across his room was engulfed in the unforgiving fire. The flames licked at the painting, spreading faster and faster as he watched. It was as if the bright morning sun Viona had painted was alive, jumping out of the mural. The paint alone was feeding the fire's hungry belly. There was no stopping it.

He watched his whole life burn up in front of him. Everything he had known. Everything he had shared with his parents. And he knew no matter how much smoke he inhaled into his lungs, and how much his eyes watered from wispy haze in the air, and the pain he felt as he watched his life burn, that he needed to get himself out of there. He needed to live.

On his elbows, he crawled to the door with his head down. He shakily stood on his knees and squeezed himself back through the door. Once through, he fell to the ground again, coughing up the thin debris inside his chest and lungs.

He lay back a moment on the ground, his eyes watering down his face uncontrollably, and he hugged the black box to his chest.

The most important things in his life were nothing that this ship could hold, and were nothing this ship could burn.

Dia told me I was famous, and that she had known about me since she was a little girl. How many other people know me, and followed my life without me knowing?

It was the first time these thoughts had ever crossed his mind.

How many people would be worried that UniX lost feed with me, or would mission control even share this information with the public?

His throat constricted and he choked, gagging into the air.

What if... I never get contact back... with them?

All of those people had a connection with him, yet he didn't know any of them. Though he'd much rather be close with a selected few than be with a lot of people and share little connection with them at all. And even though all these people felt like they shared a part in his life, none of those people knew the real Arcturus.

He grabbed at the ground before him and reached up to close the door to the AGC. The black, choking, smoke in the room was engulfing, and he needed to get out of there quick, if he was going to get out of there at all.

His head began to sway, back and forth. Back and forth. His head was light and airy, his lungs and chest full of the fumes and smoke. He clawed at his eyes, wiping back the salty water that flooded them, pleading that the stinging would subside, so he could open them. As he wiped his eye, he nicked his stitches with his hand and cried out into the compressor, inhaling deeper than he should have. His head grew lighter as his eyes rolled into the back of his head.

"Hey! Hey Arc, come hereee," a woman cooed. He heard her, but he didn't know which direction her voice was coming from. It was comforting, and he smiled, laughing to himself as he moved his head in every direction, following the sweet cadence of her voice.

"Arctuuuuurus," she called. He lifted his body and turned around, spotting a baby on his hands and knees, bouncily crawling towards the woman in his sleep room.

"Mom?" he called out, his brow furrowing at the scene. She didn't answer. She didn't even look up at him. Instead she held out her arms, smiling, and motioning her fingers for the baby to come to her arms. He brought himself to standing and backed away, staring at the baby with fright. He'd never seen a baby in real life before, and the child was tiny—a tiny human being. The baby laughed and cooed, lifting its arm to reach out for a younger, youthful, grinning Viona.

The baby pulled back and rocked back and forth on its legs, the black curly poof on its head bouncing.

His eyes widened as he stared at the baby.

It was him.

"How in the...?"

"Pretty soon you'll be walking!" she cooed at the baby, her eyes smiling at the child, a sense of pride glowing on her face.

He became mesmerized by the image before

him, and instead of watching himself as a baby, he looked at his mother.

He felt better.

Everything is going to work out.

He felt like he could make it.

"But for now, you're going to need to get to the capsule."

"Huh?" He moved forward, watching her. As she spoke to the baby, the smile on her lips, the creases on the side of her eyes melted away. Her mouth was thin, and her eyes worried. She looked from the baby directly up to Arcturus. And she stared at him, right inside him.

"Get to the capsule!"

Arcturus turned onto his side, coughing up what felt like his own lungs. He reached down and held his side, his eyes fluttering open as he looked down at the ground of the AGC. The sleep room had fully filled with smoke by now, and the flames spread, licking their way closer to him.

"Mom..." he whispered, his voice raspy.

He needed to heed her advice and get out of there, if he wanted to live.

And he did.

With all the strength he had left, he lifted himself to his shaking feet, still clutching the black box to his side in one hand. He crouched down, trying to keep low, away from the smoke. He slammed his hand over the door pad and bit his lip.

"C'monnn!" he yelled through gritted teeth.

The light turned green.

He took one last look at his sleep room as the thick, silver door began to close.

When one door closes...

The door on the other side opened. He kicked off the wall, pushing away from the door that officially closed over that period of his life.

CHAPTER THIRTEEN

Betrayal

Exhaustion ripped at his shaking muscles. Arcturus sat on the floor of the capsule, leaning his back against the secured door. He leaned over, unhitched a helmet off the side of the door, and placed it on his head with the visor down. Ahead of him was a downsized version of *Homeland's* control panel, accompanied by a massive shield. It was veiled by a thick, vinyl cover.

He used the sides of the capsule for assistance to move him around to the control panel and reached forward. He latched onto part of the thick cover and yanked it off like a sheet.

Positioning himself in front of the contoured chair, he sat, buckled himself in, and strapped down his ankles. He automatically employed the motions to power up the engine of the capsule.

It was time to separate the docked capsule from the ship, and though this had always been a familiar task, this time was different. It didn't carry the familiar feeling of an asteroid mining expedition, where he latched onto asteroids and drilled into their rough surfaces, knowing full well that at the end of a long, hard day's work, he had a warm bed to lay in, and a toilet to relieve himself with.

This time it was different because he wasn't coming back. The driving force of the fire was just too much for him to control, and it would spread.

His chair vibrated underneath him as the engine revved to life, warming itself up. He strained his eyes on the indicator bar that presented itself inside the visor of his helmet. As soon as it filled up, he hovered his hand over the touch screen of the panel.

He clenched his jaw as the separation between the capsule and *Homeland* became apparent, as if somebody were prying him away from the place he belonged. He grabbed hold of the steering mechanism and "hit the gas", also fueled by the renewable energy resource he had mined from the asteroids.

He shot away from *Homeland*.

The capsule moved with ease, as if he'd just downgraded from a diesel semi truck to a golf cart.

He powered the capsule far enough away from the burning ship into a position where he could look back upon it.

Homeland was in the distance, parallel to his line of sight.

His heart sank.

Flashing hues of blue flames danced off the inside of the graphene-lined, "hamster tube" tunnel, fighting to get out.

His eyes fixated on the ship, the gray billowing clouds of the Milky Way Galaxy blurred in the background to his left.

Homeland burned from the inside, as parts of her body broke off into the blackness. His eyes began to well up. His bottom lip quivered.

He shoved up the visor of his helmet as he swiped at his eyes. Tears floated away from him face as he watched the only home he'd ever known meet its end.

Mission control...

He remembered what started this whole thing to begin with. He'd lost feed with UniX.

"What if I ... never... " His breaths came in short spurts. His lungs were small, matching the smallness of the capsule. Panic set in his stomach as he sniffled, and he gripped onto the steering mechanism with all his might.

"I'm alone," he whispered to himself, as if saying the word aloud would remind him of his fate if he couldn't get the capsule close enough to the galaxy to regain communication.

The adrenaline born out of his fear of isolation fueled his nerves. He began to harness the void. For a moment he tried to push against his vulnerability, but it was no use. He allowed the darkness in his peripheral vision to wrap itself tightly around his body.

It was hopeless.

If he'd been out there alone before, the loss of communication with Earth had really proved that further. It showed him that even though help had been at his fingertips his whole life, they were ultimately obsolete in situations like this, situations of the unknown.

Overcome with vulnerability, he forced forward and powered up the tablet on the control panel. He reached up underneath the panel, and felt a compartment that he was familiar with, one that popped open at his touch. He pulled out a small, black earpiece. Different than the headset he wore in *Homeland*, this piece fit right into the curvature of his ear and he was able to wear it along with his helmet and visor.

He affixed it in his left ear.

"Come ooon," he urged, moving the capsule even closer, at a rate of speed that even he couldn't calculate.

Even though the QED ran completely off of entangled pairs of atoms, his logic was if he positioned the capsule back where it was before he lost feed, it would be able to power back up.

He wasn't troubleshooting all the possibilities of malfunctions the QED could be experiencing.

"Mission control, this is Ho-" He cleared his throat, his voice still raspy, and caught himself before he said the wrong ship, since he was no longer in *Homeland*.

"Mission control, this is Arcturus Holst. Do you copy? This is Arc trying to regain feed. Copy."

He tried again and again, hoping, just hoping, that they were fumbling with the channels, and they would be able to find him.

"Mission control, this i—"

The feed was silent.

He was flying solo. Blacked out and completely in the dark.

"Shit." He slammed his hands down on the edge

of the control panel, and then lifted them up as if to show the Universe he surrendered.

In his capsule overlooking the Milky Way Galaxy, he sat exhausted, confused, and frustrated. A black object caught his peripheral vision. He focused his attention on the black box, the one thing he'd saved from the fire. He reached out, resisting against the belt that strapped him to the chair and gripped his fingers around the box. He pulled it close.

When he hugged the box to his chest, he felt moving parts inside. His stomach gave a falling sensation. He turned the box slightly, hearing a clunk inside the box.

What happened? Did it fall? Is it broken?

His thoughts raced.

He turned the box upside down, studying the hitch that kept the working components of the hologram inside. He shoved his thumb into the tab and froze.

If I do this... will the memory reset?

He hesitated.

If something's moving in there... it's broken anyway, right?

He pulled up the tab with his thumb and carefully lifted it off. The back of the hologram remained in the air where he let go of it.

Looking down inside the box, all the wiring of the lights for the holograph seemed to be in place. In the back corner of the box sat a fingernail sized computer drive. The hole into the mechanics of the box was just big enough for him to squeeze his fingers in. He inched the drive along the inner wall and pulled it out, holding it up in the air to examine.

Why didn't I notice this before?

It was either secured inside the box in some way before, or he was so entranced by the image of his parents that he didn't even notice the moving part inside. Maybe the rescue mission for the box was enough to jar it loose.

As he studied the drive, he squinted his eyes to the markings on the side.

"What... is...?" He could make out several etchings. One of the letters was a curling circle, with a line that went from the middle to the outside.

"Q."

The symbol next to the Q was a figure 8, turned on its side.

"That's an infinity symbol. Q. Infinity."

Then it hit him.

His eyes widened and he straightened up in the

seat, scanning the control panel for the connector to the drive.

It hadn't even occurred to him that the reason he couldn't gain transmission with UniXplor was because he ran out of entangled pairs for the QED to function. His focus had been on distance, and the unmapped territory.

His parents planted the quantum-entangled pairs inside the hologram. They knew he'd need them.

How did they know?

"It's not possible they'd know *Homeland* would catch fire and I'd end up here! Or that'd I'd go back and save it!"

He found the connector and shoved the drive into the slot. The light on the transmitter turned green, and the silence turned to static.

His parents didn't know he'd end up in the capsule.

They knew if I was going to keep anything close to me, it'd be the box.

He reached up his hand up and rested his on his heart. His chest rose and fell with his breathing.

"Pspt." Feed from his earpiece.

A smile shot across his face.

"Misso—" He was cut off by a voice through his earpiece.

"Arc is *your* job!"

He heard his name. Leo's voice.

"I never wanted this!" It was Diamandis.

His stomach flipped at the sound of her voice, though a sense of alarm arose when he realized that she was upset. Very upset. He wanted to shout out to let them know that he had regained audio feed, though he still wouldn't be able to receive a visual until they accepted his channel feed. He wanted to shout out, "I'm here. I'm here and I'm alive!"

But he didn't.

Something told him that it was time to listen.

He unbuckled himself from the chair and allowed his feet to go backwards, hanging in the air parallel to the ceiling.

Too many times recently he'd allowed his emotions to overcome him. He wanted to regain control, even if that meant biting his tongue.

Assess the situation, Arc. Don't throw yourself into it until you know what's going on.

He pressed the earpiece harder into his ear.

"What's going on here?" He heard Lawlston coming into the room. Lawlston. He would know how to handle the situation.

What was the situation, even?

Arcturus heard Diamandis choke. Clearly she was crying. The sound of it tugged at his heartstrings. He felt for her. He wanted to comfort her, to make her feel better, to tell her that everything was going to be okay. That he was here, and that he was going to be heading back to Earth as soon as they gave him the go ahead.

"Leo made me... I couldn't keep going... I had—" She couldn't form a sentence, and continued to choke on her words, inhaling loudly to catch her breath.

"Hey, heyy. Calm down. Explain. Leo, what the hell did you make her do? She's under my command. She's my intern. We agreed she'd study under me."

"This is ridiculous," Leo scoffed at Lawlston.

"No!" Diamandis screamed. "It's not your life! You don't understand."

Arcturus was trying to gather what they were speaking about. It soon became clear why they were fighting.

"He is a *real* person. It's a human being up there! A real human with feelings, and hopes, and dreams, and when he finds out he's going to be crushed!"

Arcturus pricked his ears. He held his breath.

Do I want to know what's coming?

"What are you talking about? What's wrong with A—" Lawlston began, when he was cut off by Leo's slick voice once more.

He's not going to find out." Leo said quietly, sternly.

"Someone speak now," Lawlston demanded.

"Leo's forced me to get to know Arcturus on an intimate level. He told me to engage him in a relationship to pique his interest in a return mission, since he was worried he'd... " She seemed more composed than she did before, almost as if she replaced her tears with anger, and needed to catch a breath. She continued, "... Worried that he'd lose interest when his parents passed," she finished.

Arcturus began to panic.

Panic.

He couldn't believe what he was hearing, and the walls of the capsule began to spin, orbiting around his vision and closing in on him. He began to lose his breath. But he had to keep listening.

"Really, how intimate can you get?" Leo degraded.

She burst out again. "We had sex, Leo! I went in over my head before I realized what we were doing was wrong!" she yelled.

"For God sake, you had sex? You can't have sex

with somebody halfway across the galaxy!" Leo laughed out loud, which sent painful chills of anger up Arcturus' spine.

A burning sensation overtook his body. He was hot, sweaty, and betrayed.

How? How could she use me?

Not just her but the entire mission team used him and played with his emotions to get what they wanted.

His head shot over to the tablet, which instantly lit up. The screen flashed up an image of the control room on Earth. Diamandis and Leo stood in the middle of the room. Her stance was defensive, her arms crossed over her chest.

"Why would you do this?" Lawlston spoke deeply, from the corner of the room. It was then that Arcturus realized Lawlston held down the button that accepted feed with his capsule.

How long did Lawlston know I was here? Why did he wait until this very moment to reconfigure to QED and bring me into this room?

Arcturus fluttered his eyes as the heat blackened his sight. He exhaustedly dropped his gaze on the golden blond hair of Diamandis.

"Oh my... No! No—Arc! It's honestly not what you think!" she yelled, running up to the screen with her arms raised, pleading and begging him to listen to her.

His eyes glazed over. He couldn't even begin to fathom forming words. He opened his mouth to speak, but his throat was dry, and sore. His face was singed from the smoke, his heart felt smashed to pieces.

I was set up? This girl was put into my life to 'make' me fall in love with her?

For the purpose of the mission, and the mission only.

Leo raised his hands in the air and dropped them lazily by his side, rolling his eyes.

"I knew it was a damn mistake investing all this money in the mission. Your mother had an idea of her own, and we've had to deal with you your entire life and your unpredictable mood swings pulling my money every which way!" Leo shot his mouth off, ignoring Diamandis' emotions as she collapsed into a chair, bawling into her hands and creating a smeary mess, inhaling as though she couldn't catch her breath. Arcturus watched her as Leo spoke, not quite sure how he felt about her dismay. At this point he was numb.

"Oh come on now, Leo!" Lawlston stepped forward. "This mission wasn't a mission without Viona, and you know it. She knew what she was doing, and she's broken barriers for science that no human ever has." He spoke swiftly and clearly. Then he turned to Arcturus and stared through the screen, into his capsule.

"And you have, too. Don't let anyone take that away from you," he finished off sternly.

Arcturus looked from Lawlston back to Diamandis.

"You're right about one thing," he spoke, his voice cracked and raspy, directly at Leo.

Diamandis lifted her head, her eyes puffy and smeared, her lips slightly parted.

Leo stepped forward as Arcturus finished his sentence.

"I *have* lost interest in a return mission." His voice was monotone, and he stared into the screen at their reactions, his eyelids heavy and covering half his eyes behind his helmet visor.

Diamandis leaped to her feet. "Arc, no!! Please let me ex—"

"I'm done talking to you." He lifted his hand up to silence her, not looking in her direction.

She pursed her lips, her eyes wide and filled with tears. Her face turned red.

"I'm glad to see that all of you have noticed before this meeting, that I am the one that has control over this mission. And there's nothing you or your money can do about it." He spoke more directly to Leo this time.

The silence in the room was poison, and now it was their turn to be speechless.

Lawlston stepped forward. "Arc, this is crucial. As your doctor, you need to allow me to take a look at you. I can clearly see you've been through a lot, and I—"

Arcturus cut him off. "I'm okay with a different feed." He said quietly, eyeing the betrayers.

"Zone 7."

"I'm not in *Homeland* anymore, there are no zones. Find me on the receiver."

CHAPTER FOURTEEN

Capsule

Arcturus leaned forward and turned off the visual on his tablet, blacking out the screen as he reached up and switched off the receiver on his audio. He pushed back from the panel and sighed heavily, consciously noticing his tense muscles as he wallowed in his own vulnerability.

What am I supposed to do with this information?

This changed everything.

The thing that stabbed him in the side the most painfully was the fact that Diamandis was a lie.

She made me... hopeful.

His body ached all over. Before he could do anything else, he flipped the receiver and audio onto a different feed, waiting for Lawlston to find him.

Maybe it would be okay if Lawlston never found my feed.

Soon enough, the screen was flashing and the receiver brought up an image of an examination room, Lawlston adjusting the front of the camera. He backed up, touching his ear as if he was applying an earpiece microphone. "I'm sorry you had to go through that," he said quietly, his lips finely lined inside his closely shaven goatee.

Arcturus nodded, and then shrugged his shoulders. He was sorry too.

"Why aren't you in *Homeland*?" He got straight to the point, as if he was trying to get Arcturus' mind off the situation, but also trying to see how he could help. "And I'm also not sure why we lost feed, but you look beat. Can you take off your helmet for me?" He asked, his medical examining voice resurfacing.

Arcturus reached up and carefully removed the helmet, smashing down his hair before letting it go to drift around the capsule.

"Your face is singed. There was a fire?" Lawlston asked, his face concerned, his eyes squinted forward at the scene.

"When I moved *Homeland* further away from The Milky Way, I believed I... " He took a break and breathed in and out, closing his eyes a moment before continuing on. "Went out of the reception range. So I tried to steer back, but the mechanism was stuck, wouldn't let me steer. I went to the back of the ship to see, but the entire thing was in flames. Not sure where it started," he finished, closing his eyes once more.

"Do you have food?" Lawlston asked, his eyebrow rising.

"I grabbed that one tub in the control room."

Lawlston exhaled.

"That's good. That's good. But you may need to cut your supply down to twice a day instead of three, so you can conserve."

"I figured." Arcturus sighed; the thought of his stomach aching even more than it did now from being hungry was the last thing he wanted to think about right now.

"But if you have some of that aloe spread in there, I would use it on the skin on your face that you've singed, as well as your eyelashes. It will help provide nutrients to your skin."

Arcturus nodded again.

"Does anything else hurt?" Lawlston asked.

"My entire body aches. And I was having... " He hesitated.

Viona was crouching down and calling his name,

flames rising up behind her.

"Well when I was trying to get out of there... I passed out. And I think I started hallucinating."

"What did you see?"

"My mom. She told me I needed to get to the capsule if I wanted to live."

"And you did."

"Huh?" Arcturus asked, trying to keep up.

"You did want to live." Lawlston replied. "It's normal to have hallucinations when you've experienced smoke inhalation. And it's normal to see a loved one once they've passed. But you saved yourself, Arc. You are the only one who has that kind of control." He smiled.

Arcturus studied his face, his brow furrowed. He wasn't sure he liked that answer.

"You need to talk to her."

"My mom?" he asked, slightly confused.

"Diamandis," Lawlston clarified.

"Why would I do that?" he questioned, offended.

"Because you owe it to—"

"I don't owe anyone anything."

"You didn't let me finish. Because you owe it to yourself. She meant something to you."

Arcturus sat back in the chair, his capsule hovering in the darkness outside the galaxy. *Homeland* was merely a skeleton by now. He reached up and pulled out the earpiece underneath his helmet, returning it to its place by the control panel.

He instantly felt the repercussions of lack of sleep. Exhaustion washed over him, and his entire being was drained. There was a pain in his eyes when he rolled them around in their sockets, making visuals out of his peripheral vision very difficult. He unbuckled himself from the chair and allowed himself to float up, using what strength he had left to paddle into the middle of the capsule.

His new home was small. He could stretch his arms out straight to both sides, and there were about 3 feet on both sides before he hit a wall. He pulled himself into a ball and hugged his knees together, staying very still in the air. He closed his eyes tightly.

He didn't want to talk to her. He wasn't ready. Lawlston respected his request to have some time to think before his emotions fueled his actions. He didn't know what he would say to her.

After his initial feelings anger and betrayal, his mind was immediately filled with a sense of vulnerability. He felt stupid for believing that she actually wanted to be with him.

The boy from space. The boy who would return to planet Earth for the first time when he's an old man.

He laughed out loud.

It was stupid of me to actually believe I had a chance. I'm stupid.

Beep.

The receiver on the control panel was blinking green.

It was time.

Arcturus straightened himself out and leaned forward. He hovered his hand over the button a moment. Then he pressed it.

He watched the screen of the tablet as the empty medical examination room came into view. He tapped his foot against the edge of the chair, the nerves beginning to tingle through his body. Though he had tried to get some sleep before mission control connected back with him, he couldn't.

There was too much on his mind.

He looked around at the white room, a shiver running up his spine at the sterility of it. He, himself, still felt numbness inside, and he wasn't sure if he'd ever be able to heal from it. The door creaked open, he watched Diamandis walk in, closing the door behind her, her back to him.

His throat began to close up.

There she was again.

What's going to happen?

Was she going to come in crying on her knees and begging him to forgive her, or was she going to be calm and collected and take what she felt she deserved?

She turned around, and Arcturus' heart flipped over when he saw her face. She looked terrible, with big bags under her eyes. She'd been crying. She had her hair pulled back, and her cheeks had lost their usual rosy glow. Her eyes were sad, sympathetic.

She opened her mouth to speak, and her words came out softly, her voice cracked. "Won't you please just let me explain?" she breathed, moving herself closer to the screen, and she pulled herself up onto the exam table, the paper crinkling underneath her.

"S'why I'm here." He spoke dryly.

"I didn't want things to end up like this. I really care for you, Arc."

"You don't have to do that." He closed his eyes,

shaking his head. "I'm tired of the lies."

"No! I'm not lying. Yes, it started out because the heads of UniXplor approached me. They were afraid that you needed more motivation—"

"I heard."

She stopped, sighing, and looking away from the screen. "I feel so horrible," she said, placing her hand on her stomach. "Everything changed when I met you, Arcturus. You have to believe that," she pleaded with him. "I had no idea what I was getting myself into. I had no idea that you were going to be… so real."

"Really, Dia. I don't need this. I've had enough." He spoke quickly, quietly.

I shouldn't have done this. I shouldn't have spoken to her again.

"I've already felt the deepest pain of betrayal."

She hopped off the exam table and moved closer to the screen, about to open her mouth to protest, but Arcturus was faster.

"Not just from you, from the entire team. I don't need you to try and make me feel better."

She exhaled. "I'm not." Her eyes began to well again. She reached her hand up to her cheek, and he noticed it was trembling.

"The thing is," he began, relaxing the tense muscles in his neck and shoulders. "I realize that all of this... all of us, may have been just a fantasy."

"No—"

"Just listen. But even if it was only fantasy, I really felt something for you. And even though I wish I could have more of that feeling, of feeling like I'm wanted by someone, anyone. Of feeling like I'm actually part of something greater in my life, and that I'm not just a science experiment used for the benefit of everyone but myself... even though I wish I could experience that again, I know that it's over."

Diamandis put her hand over her mouth. She muffled her whimpering. "I... I don't know what else to say," she whispered when she was able to gather herself.

"You don't have to say anything," he whispered back, quiet, and he avoided her gaze. "But... did you feel any ounce of love for me?" he asked.

"Yes," she answered quickly, confidently. "Do you believe me?"

Arcturus sat for a moment, and just concentrated on his breathing.

Take in this moment.

He looked up into her swirling, icy blue, sparkling eyes and nodded his head yes.

He thought he could see the corner of her lips twitch into a small smile.

She spoke softly, "One can hope, right?"

He stared at the black screen of the tablet, as if a picture of Diamandis had been burned into the display.

It was painful to breathe, and he couldn't tell if it was from heartbreak, or a physical medical condition. He let his head fall limp, taking his eyes off the tablet. As he relaxed his neck, his chin to his chest, he stared down at his suit. He noticed a blob of red floating in the air, away from his face. He looked up, realizing it was coming from his face. He held his hand up to head and dabbed at the stitches, looking down at his fingers.

Nothing.

Then he felt a tickling sensation under his nose. He unconsciously reached up and swiped it, more droplets of blood expelling into the atmosphere around him.

"Ah, shit," he cursed, and lifted the sleeve of his arm up to his nose to put pressure on it. He pulled it away; the crimson had seeped into the fabric of his suit. He really didn't care if he'd ruined yet another suit, it seemed as though this one was pretty much shot anyway.

On top of all his injuries, a nosebleed was yet another one he needed to add to the list, and he was going to ignore the list in the end anyway.

This is something I will not report to Lawlston...

Lawlston.

He was the only one left that Arcturus felt he could really trust.

But can I?

What was Lawlston's reason for wanting Arcturus to hear the conversation between Leo and Diamandis? Had his doctor and mentor never pressed that button, would Arcturus have revealed to Diamandis that he knew the truth? How much further would she have taken their relationship? How much further would she have played with his emotions? The worst part about it all, was that if she never knew that he knew she was assigned to make him fall in love with her, would he have allowed the fantasy to continue, just for the company? Would he in turn, use her?

That's not how it played out. It happened to way it was supposed to. And I'm alone.

Did he like it better that way?

He pulled his sleeve back and looked around at his surroundings. The space was a lot smaller than he was used to, and he wasn't sure he even wanted to get used to that. He looked from all the keys and buttons on the control panel out the large window at the view of the Milky Way Galaxy, to all the steel drawers in the capsule that he only needed to use for work before.

Worst of all, there was no bathroom in there. He knew this because when he went on his exterior expeditions to mine asteroids, he had to hold it until he got back to the ship. He didn't even want to think about the next time he'd need to relieve himself. He'd have to deal with diapers the whole time he'd spend in here. He hoped on his life, that there *were* diapers stashed in here somewhere.

He looked out at the Milky Way Galaxy again, thinking about the many lives on planet Earth that were counting on him to save the future of mankind. But what were they looking for? He knew exactly what this mission was about. Whereas it may have started as something different to his parents, Arcturus knew that the good intentions of breaking a human record, and curiosity of the cosmos is what started the mission, but it seemed to have turned into him modeling as the contractor, looking for a new and improved space to occupy and exploit for their own benefit.

Arcturus searched around the capsule for the black box again. He found it wedged into the corner, and he flattened his body in order to grab it out of the air and hold it to himself.

He moved up and pushed himself against the wall, leaving room in the middle of the capsule for the Hologram to take up the space. He pressed the button, and held his breath.

Please.

He hoped it still worked after retrieving the entangled pairs drive from it earlier. The line of light streamed from the small black box, projecting Viona and Dex, the same image as before, into the middle of the room. He sighed with relief.

He flipped a button on the side of the box, silencing the volume of them speaking to him. He wanted to imagine that they were really in the room with him, rather than hearing a repeat of what they said before for his 30th birthday. He didn't want the reality that they were just an illusion, a hologram.

How did they see the outcome of their mission?

He remembered putting on his father's white flight suit, the one Dex wore when they launched from Earth thirty-one years ago. He thought about how happy his mother had been when she saw him wearing it, bringing her back to that particular day. She was so happy and so proud of all her accomplishments.

Arcturus watched the visual of his parents look at each other and laugh, talking to each other, and then to him through the projection.

"What would you do, Mom?" he said out loud. Listening to the sound of his own voice brought him comfort, knowing that it was still a form of exercising communication, regardless if anyone could hear him or not.

"The mission has gone so far off course from what you were dreaming... " he whispered, guilt flooding his exhausted limbs. He knew that there was no way he could bring it back to what she would have wanted, which was exploring space as means of learning more about their own blue planet.

"What do I do?" he pleaded, hoping that somebody else would give him the answer, instead of having to search for it himself.

He watched the hologram finish, his mother saying her final words, before it started over again.

And in that instance, a small inkling of a smile came to his lips, and he realized that the answer had been in front of him this whole time.

He reached out and flipped the 'off' button on the black box, shutting down the hologram. The light cleared and sharpened his view through the window to the outside of Milky Way, into the Universe. He swam over to the chair in front of the control panel reached down, and pulled a lever. The release allowed the top and bottom of the chair to lay flat into a makeshift cot.

He was about to maneuver himself onto the bed when a blinking light appeared on the control panel before him, indicating an incoming communication with mission control. He stared at the blinking button, reached up and turned it off.

"Later... " he whispered to the tablet, and he turned to curl himself up into a ball on the makeshift cot. He needed to rest to be able to regain his strength and allow his exhausted muscles to heal. He needed to rest up, because he had work to do.

CHAPTER FIFTEEN

Coming Home

A rcturus lifted the hand mirror up in the air, observing his reflection. He reached up and touched his eyebrow. The stitches were out, and the gash had healed up nicely, despite the fact that he was undoubtedly going to have a scar there for the rest of his life. It would forever remind him of when he got it, coming back into *Homeland* after his mother's funeral.

The singed, raw skin on his face had also almost fully replaced itself, healing over with new skin after he heeded Lawlston's advice to apply the aloe from one of his food pouches.

He lifted his hands off the mirror and left it to drift, rotating his body around in the lack of gravity. He'd organized all the materials he brought with him from *Homeland* along with the things that were in there before, so he could maximize what little space he did have. It wasn't as bad as he thought it was going to be, considering he'd downgraded from a very large ship to living full time in the capsule. And on top of that, the capsule didn't have the capacity to harbor any of the paragravity hardware that was developed for *Homeland*, so he was battling weightlessness the entire time.

Since it was only him, he didn't mind the lack of space. He could look out at the vastness of the Universe before him, and see the possibilities of hostility. For now, he was safe here.

After the events that happened with mission control, Arcturus spent the following few Earth weeks planning his next move. He finished out the extensive tasks mission control instructed him to perform, including a plan written out by Viona. He also had plenty of time to map out his plan of action for surviving in the capsule; food, recycled water, and the situation with his waste. The only thing he had left was to transfer the files to UniX before the return mission.

He floated over to the panel, grabbed a headset he found in a drawer to the left of the panel chair, which he preferred over the earpiece, and placed it over his hair. He then adjusted the tablet, and pressed a few indicators to reach connectivity with Earth.

"Mission control this is Arcturus calling from *Homebound.*"

He'd come up with a name for his new home, and found the name quite fitting for the little capsule.

"Mission control, come in." The screen was fuzzy, but it soon gained a clear picture of the great room that held all the computers.

"Hey, Arc!" one of the engineers called out from behind a desk.

"Hello," he said, looking around the room to see if he saw anyone that he needed to direct this call to.

"Looking for...?"

"Well Leo, I guess." Arcturus bit his lip. "Well. No. It doesn't matter. I just wanted to send you guys the last chip." He reached into the pocket of the front of his jumpsuit, and pulled out a small microchip that fit between his thumb and index finger.

"Oh you can send that right over. Let me go get admin for you," The engineer stood up and hurried towards the door. "... don't go anywhere!"

Arcturus looked over both of his shoulders before replying to the engineer, "Not many places to run off to..."

He slid the chip into a port on the control panel.

"... And he came in on this zone?" He heard Leo's voice as he and the engineer entered the room. Leo stopped in his tracks when he looked at the screen.

"You're doing a transfer?" he asked, narrowing his eyes.

At first Arcturus didn't speak. He wasn't sure if he wanted to have a conversation with this guy. He wasn't sure if he had healed from their last encounter.

He had a job to do, and whether or not he was angry at this admin, he needed to get things done his way.

"I'm transferring the majority of the files of my findings and conducted experiments aboard *Homebound*, since I've evacuated *Homeland*." He held his composure; his body hovered weightlessly in the capsule.

"Great!" Leo shouted, moving behind a computer and remaining standing, he bent down and began to type into it.

"Wilser, you have the receiver going?" he called over to another employee behind a desk.

"Why is the file size so..." he began, when Arcturus finished his sentence before he could.

"I can bring the holographic data and 3-D video

back to you in person. I figured I'd send a big head start on some of the numerical data and small photos that my mom and I worked on right before we exited Milky Way. That will give you a lot of material to sift through over the next few years, as it took us several years to conduct and collect it."

"Lawlston will be pleased to hear you will attempt to come back. We've already been working on plans for a retrieval mission the second we heard about *Homeland*. Too bad Lawlston won't be around to see it. He's getting old." Leo's eyes were intense.

He just won't let up!

Fire licked Arcturus' insides as he watched Leo's facial expressions, though he couldn't help but feel calm.

He had full control over the outcome of this mission. He raised his hand in the air, mimicking a fake toasting glass, something he'd seen people in movies do as a cultural thing.

"Here's to you dying before I return as well." Arcturus' voice was dry and monotone, his eyes pressed like stone. He smirked.

Leo didn't like that.

Leo looked down, ignoring Arcturus as he typed into the keyboard. He looked over to the side at one of his employees sitting at a computer and spoke to them. "Make sure you secure the transfer on the files or you can pack your things. They are very important."

Arcturus closed his eyes, shaking his head back and forth. How this guy got the job as admin after Zander died was beyond him, unless it was nepotism.

It had to have been an inside job. Either that, or my parents were being played the whole time, until their deaths, where the admin thought he could get away with anything. Thinking he could get away with whatever he wants and I wouldn't do anything about it.

He was wrong.

"Are you beginning the return mission home?" Leo asked the screen.

Arcturus stared in at his stupid, spiked, blond hair.

"I have to document it. And I better let Lawlston know because he'll want to check your vitals upon re-entry." Leo was being mildly reasonable for the moment, but only because he had to follow procedure.

"Tonight. I'm beginning my *Homebound* mission tonight." Arcturus spoke clearly.

"Right... until then." Leo tipped his imaginary

hat, mocking Arcturus' attempt at trying to belong to any cultural norm with the toasting glass act. He straightened his back and headed for the door.

"Leo!" Arcturus shouted out to him as he reached for the door. He turned and looked over his shoulder, a greedy smirk pasted on his face. "Make sure you view all the files very thoroughly. We spent a lot of time on them. *Thoroughly*."

Without another word, Leo had the door open, and he was through it.

CHAPTER SIXTEEN

Breathe

His heart was pounding out of his chest.

Thump-thump, thump-thump.

A sticky heat formed at his hairline and around the back of his neck. He grabbed onto the sides of the chair, knowing full well controlling the steering was beyond him now. He did all he could to guide the capsule. At this point, it was all up to the atmosphere to finish the job and slow him down.

The capsule was moving at high speeds, which was normal, though he had never experienced this motion before. Now, he felt every jolt of the spacecraft, every bump, and every chip that peeled from the paint on the exterior.

He was immobile in his large, puffy, exterior space suit, making his muscles feel as though they were moving in slow motion. He wore a new helmet, much larger than the broken one. Connected at the back of his helmet was a set of tubes leading to an oxygen tank that lay flat against his back.

Before he began to make his descent onto the blue and green planet with white swirly clouds hovering, he decided to suit up for an exterior expedition, because he didn't know what was to come.

His stomach tied up in knots, he became more and more nervous as he watched the altitude meter go further and further down in numbers, something he'd never witnessed before firsthand.

He braced himself and kept his eyes peeled on the front window at the land fast approaching.

At the land.

He didn't know what to expect, whether or not he'd crash on ground or water, or if *Homebound* would catch on fire, or even explode all together. He didn't know if he would die upon impact, or land with ease.

Or even if someone would be there to greet him.

This is a huge risk.

This seemed to be a pattern in his life.

I have nothing to lose.

He clenched his muscles, balling his hands into

fists. His body and mind juddered back and forth, his vision blurring.

He squeezed his eyes shut until he saw black and blue.

The sound was deafening.

His eyelids turned from blue to red as the inside of the capsule lit up from the natural light of the planet. He slowly opened his eyes, blinking his sight back.

He looked out the window at the world he'd landed on.

I am breathing. I am alive. I am breathing!

His body was positioned sideways on the chair, and he remained strapped in. Out the window, he saw what looked like asteroids to him, except they were planted on the ground. Above the rocks, he followed the window up to what must have been the sky. It was a light blue, with swirling white puffs. The lighting was dim, as though it was beginning to be nighttime on this planet.

As soon as the high-pitched scream in his ears subsided, he scrambled. He bent down and pulled the straps off his ankles, unbuckling himself from the chair he sat in. Once he unbuckled himself, he fell to the wall, which was currently the floor. His suit provided enough padding so it didn't hurt, and he crawled along the wall to get to the door of the capsule.

He continued to keep his helmet on, worried that he wouldn't be able to breathe when he exited *Homebound*. He'd seen people do it in movies and his parents told him stories about their lives many times. He knew that people didn't live in spacesuits their whole lives, but he wasn't sure nonetheless.

He held onto the handle of the door, and closing his eyes a moment, he pulled down on the lever. He took a deep breath, pushing the door open with all his strength, the door swinging back and hitting the outside of the capsule. Holding onto the door, a beam of natural light shot through to the back of the capsule.

Arcturus' body swayed, and he felt light headed. Regardless he began to try to take a step. He lifted his foot forward, realizing the distance between the capsule door and the ground.

As he let go, his legs felt like jello, and they buckled underneath him. He fell out of the door-way of the capsule and onto the rocks below with an "Umph!"

He rolled over, moaning from the fall, and flipped

over on his stomach. His breathing began to increase as his heart pounded.

He felt exhilarated to be alive, and on the water planet at last.

Why won't my legs work?

He groaned.

He used his arms and elbows to crawl, dragging his legs behind him. He scooted up onto the land and when he got to a level surface, he laid flat.

Did anybody see me fall out of the sky?

He spent a long time researching this planet upon arrival. It had water. It had oxygen. There were a lot of things he didn't know about it, but he wanted to find out.

Most importantly, he strategically saved some matched pairs for the QED. For the faces of the ones on Earth he truly cared about.

Lawlston. Even Diamandis. Everyone who helped him grow throughout his life from the other side of the screen.

He could contact them and tell them he was alive…

But.

Despite his disorientation, he reached up to his helmet and placed both palms on the visor.

It was time.

He unhitched his helmet.

He ripped it off, his lungs filling with the air around him. He inhaled deeply and began to choke, which quickly subsided as he laid his cheek against the ground.

He began to laugh inside, allowing it to bubble up and out of him.

"Home... " He whispered.

"I'm home!"

CHAPTER SEVENTEEN

The Space Boy

The crowd hushed as the head of UniXplor took the podium. He was young, probably in his thirties, with long black hair that was sleek and straight. He was carefully trimmed, and wearing a suit and tie for the occasion. He face was kind, as if one could stop and have a conversation with him and feel as though they had always been friends.

The crowd roared up in applause as he hesitated a moment, and then walked up to the podium in the middle of the stage, the big UniXplor banner stretched across behind him.

"Ladies and Gentlemen. It is with great honor that I come to you to deliver this speech. I have been honored to lead UniXplor and its missions after the unexpected retirement of Dr. Leo Zander." He paused a moment, clearing his throat.

"Many years ago, UniXplor embarked on a mission that was near impossible before. Two passionate explorers, astronomers, and great scientists dedicated their lives to space exploration and made this mission possible. Many of you know Viona and Dex Holst gave up their lives for the betterment of the human race, and signed up for a mission they knew they would never return from.

"And many of you know what comes next. They devised a plan to not only create a successful mission with different experiments needed for space, science, and medicine, but they also devised a plan to bring back their ship, *Homeland*. And that was by birthing a son.

"Arcturus Holst guided us through deep space, all the way to the exterior of our very own Milky Way Galaxy. He conquered so many firsts! First human born in space, first child to be raised outside of Earth, first human to leave our galaxy. And he would be the first human to step foot for the first time on our planet as an old man in his sixties. And we will welcome him as one of our own, one who has broken ground further than anyone before! He's lost his family, but we can't allow him to feel that he is lost!"

The crowd began to roar, cheering and clapping, thrilled about the words they were hearing.

"Here to tell you about the rest of the mission, is a man who knew Arcturus better than anyone on this Earth. He was with him when he was born, and took care of him as ground support throughout his entire life. Please give a warm welcome to Dr. Hinder Lawlston."

The crowd cheered as Lawlston took the stage, and using a cane, he slowly made his way closer to the head of UniXplor. His back was hunched, and his hair fully white, the wrinkles on his face showed every line of the age he endured. He reached the podium and grabbed onto the sides, stabilizing himself against it as he looked out into the crowd. He squinted, lights from afar blinding him on the stage so much that he couldn't see the crowds of people that lined the lawn to hear the fate of the boy in space.

Lawlston nodded at the head admin, who stepped off the stage and stood in the wing, ready to listen to the old man speak.

"Thank you, Dr. Roder, thank you," he spoke out to the wing, before turning to the crowd.

"I don't even know where to begin. Uhh... " he paused, taking a shaky breath. The crowd was silent, as if each individual were holding on to his words.

"I guess I'll start at the beginning." He looked up, ready for opposition, but the entirety of the crowd remained silent. Completely hushed, all eyes were on him.

"I never wanted to be a part of this mission. The suicide mission of sending humans into space to explore the outside of our Milky Way Galaxy. I was thrown into a pool of doctors and surgeons, and selected based on credentials and experience. I wanted nothing to do with this... Until I met a young lady named Viona Holst. When I met with her for the first time, she shared with me her passion for the cosmos. As I watched her explain to me her plans for the mission, I could see a glimmer in her eyes. She knew it was suicide. She knew that she was going to die out there, and she still wanted nothing more than to go on that mission. She was supported by her husband Dex, who only wanted to be with her, and she convinced me just enough of all the good, and hope, that this mission would bring for Earth."

Lawlston took a breather, reaching underneath the podium for a glass of water that sat there for him. With shaking hands, he took a gulp, wetting his throat. The place was silent as he closed his eyes and drank before putting the cup back underneath on the shelf of the silver steel podium.

"Viona became like a daughter to me, and she not only convinced me, she convinced all the world that this mission would save the future of mankind. She hoped to explore outside our galaxy, to better learn more about the world we live in here. That was her mission. I learned before she and Dex launched that they had gotten pregnant. On purpose. It was a very big risk, but she wouldn't let me mentor her on what I thought about it. She was going to have it her way, and nobody was going to stop her.

"That's when Arcturus came along. I watched that little boy grow through the screen. Now the public did get an insight into the life of the Holst family, but there's no way that all of you could know what that family went through up there in space. Viona's mission began to turn, and she died before she got the opportunity to realize this. It was the boy, Arcturus, named after the lonely red giant, the brightest star in the Northern Celestial Hemisphere that discovered when the mission changed. It went from an exploration dedicated to learning more about our own planet, to an exploitation of the cosmos when we humans exhaust this planet. And for that reason...

he is already lost far beyond and there's nothing we can do to bring him back. I am here today, to show you what Arcturus has discovered, while the rest of us were blind."

Lawlston grabbed his cane and began to walk towards the wing, his back hunched. Roder came out from the side and grabbed the old man's wrist to guide him. The two of them whispered to each other.

"I'll get the projector started for you, don't worry about it, you can go back up there. Yeah don't worry about it." Roder assured Lawlston.

Lawlston spun around and shuffled his way back up to the podium.

A light shone up above him on the wall behind, where the UniXplor banner hung. A white screen began to lower down from the ceiling of the amphitheater and the light from the screen behind the crowd somewhere projected on the screen.

"While Leo, myself, and the team were going over the extensive amounts of research that the Holsts developed in *Homeland*, we came across a file that was different from the rest. It was hidden, but he wanted us to find it. We have watched it, and I, myself, have watched it so many times I could repeat back to you word for word what he needed to express. We have finally decided that it is time to share this with the public. And so you'll know." Lawlston began to scoot to the edge again with his cane, hoping there would be a chair in the wing for him—not just because his age did not allow him the strength to stand for long periods of time, but also because the video winded him every time he watched it, as if he was experiencing it for the first time all over again.

The lights dimmed, and for the first time he was able to see all the people in the crowd. As the video began to play, he searched the crowd. And as the light from the projection reflected back on the crowd, his attention dove right to the center, where he spotted her. And he knew she would come. He knew she wouldn't miss it. And for a moment his heart ached even more, if possible.

Arcturus appeared on the screen, floating inside the small capsule as he looked at the camera. He looked healthy, with his curly black hair a little longer than usual, poofed to the ceiling from the lack of gravity in his capsule. His eyes were vibrant, and the scar on his eyebrow healed, the black thread he stitched up completely gone. His cheeks were rosy, and he had the start of a very thick, black beard forming around his mouth.

"Greetings, Earthlings," he spoke, his voice low and smooth. He cracked a smile.

"I am coming to you from my new home, which I call *Homebound*." He lifted his hands up, looking around the capsule.

"My name is Arcturus Holst, and I was the first human born in space."

His face wore a serious expression, his mouth thin beneath his beard, and his eyes fixed on the camera, as if his stare could pierce through the screen into the eyes of everyone that watched it.

"I am here to tell you there will be no return mission."

The crowd existed in a tense silence.

"I am tired. I was born and raised in *Homeland*, the ship UniXplor created for the mission outside Milky Way Galaxy. My mother Viona was a great woman. She taught me everything I know today, and regardless of the fact that I knew I would never live a normal life, she was there for me, understanding and crying with me every step of the way, until she died. My father, Dex, was the one that taught me the technical side, and the survival tools I have needed to carry on with the mission after his death. He loved my mom, and he loved me. But he left us first, and it was my mom and I that had to carry out our duties for UniXplor upon *Homeland* when he was gone.

Even though I will always have my parents here," He held his hand up to his chest.

"I am alone now. Everyone knew that this day would come, when my parents would pass and I would be here alone until my return mission. And though I will carry with me everything I was taught growing up, I feel like I have learned the most about myself now that I am here, in this part of my life.

And so I'm confident in saying... " He paused a moment, redirecting his attention. He grabbed onto the back of the chair to get ready.

"Screw this entire mission." His eyes were furious. "Specifically Leo, the head admin of UniXplor, you have seen my entire life as a science project, and it is *you* who failed everyone in this mission. I'm done playing your games, and it is time for you to finally realize that I have always had the upper hand. And Lawlston... " He paused, catching his bearings, his face retracting back to a softness. "I'm sorry, man. You were, and always will be a second father to me." His voice was low and quiet and Arcturus paused, taking a break for a moment, getting his bearings before he could speak again.

"If I could give one message to all of you, it would be this. Be grateful and take care of what you have. It is far more rewarding to know that you've worked hard for what you have, rather than tossing it out for the next best thing. My mother had a plan, a mission, and I am not failing her by not returning. Instead, I am moving forward. I've realized now that I don't need to live on the land you did to benefit from the same values. I am a real person, and I have real feelings. It's the relationships in my life that have made it worth living, that have helped me to grow.

But I have never been a part of your world. I have never stepped foot on Earth, and living in solitude until I'm an old man is not the life for me. Instead I will fight for my existence. You should fight for your existence, too. If you learn one thing from me, from the mission, please let it be the true value of your inner self.

But for me, Earth has never been, and never will be my home."

Arcturus reached up and placed both his index finger and his middle finger together on the center of his lips, his eyes staring directly into the camera lens.

The feed cut.

Before the lights came back on, Lawlston watched her in the crowd. At the last statement, Diamandis lifted her fingers up to her lips and motioned the same thing Arcturus did.

She had fallen to her knees, crying out as though something above her had taken control. The crowd broke into a circle around her.

She knew they would never really be *with* each other, and that was what made her fall apart. But in that moment, Diamandis knew she should have fought for him, for them. She knew she wouldn't be able to wait for him, living with the hope of the fantasy inside her computer screen. She knew she would move on with her life, find a new lover and perhaps have a family. But all of this came with the thought that someday she would be able to hold the face of the space boy she once loved with her full heart. What pained her most was the fact that Arcturus would believe it had been her job to make him fall in love with her, which he did. But she did too. And the fact that he motioned a kiss that she knew was directed only to her, she knew that she could go on living, knowing that he may or may not have known the truth in the end.

Many years ago, before Leo retired and before she was demoted from the mission because of her unprofessional involvement with it, she caught wind of a rescue mission. The information was classified, if there was anything happening at all.

But if there was one thing she learned from her distant love, it was nothing other than hope.

And she would always have a special place for him in her heart. If she ever wanted to see Arcturus, all she needed to do was look to the stars.

THE END

BOOKS BY
KRISTIN HELLING

Books available where all books are sold.

THE IDEA MAN TRILOGY
(comedic, suspense thriller)
The Idea Man
The Marked Man
The True Man

THE MASTERMIND
MURDERERS SERIES
(psychological, crime thriller) *The Altruism Effect*
The Bystander Effect
The Carbon Effect
The Domino Effect

STANDALONE SERIES
(soft sci fi Thriller)
Capsule

About the Author

KRISTIN HELLING enjoys stories with a journey- whether it's across the globe, through space, or a journey of finding ones self.

She is married to a photographer, a Mama, and owns a coffeehouse outside of Kansas City, Missouri.

Kristin has been writing and publishing books since 2013, but this is the first novel she published.

If you liked *Capsule* and want more from Kristin Helling, head over to www.kristinhelling.com and join her mailing list!